Unprecedented Times

An Anthology by the
Monash Writers Group

Tale

National Library of Australia Cataloguing-in-Publication entry
Creator: Monash Writers Group, author.
Title: Unprecedented Times: Monash Writers Anthology.
ISBN: 978-0-6480386-2-7 (paperback)
Subjects: short stories.
Cover design by Karen Scott.
Cover images from Shutterstock.

Tale Publishing
Melbourne Victoria

Other Anthologies by the Monash Writers Group

The Last Line
The First Line
View from the Hill

Contents

Introduction

Welcome to the Monash Writers Group's fourth anthology. Our last two anthologies had themes based on the first or last line of a story. In 2020, we felt that the state of the world was too hard to ignore when choosing this year's theme. However, we also didn't want to tie our anthology too much to Covid-19. After all, the year began with major bushfires in Australia where an area larger than Norway was burnt out – so we rejected ideas such as *Virus*, *Lockdown* and *Plague*. Instead, we chose the more open theme of *Unprecedented Times*. Consequently, we have stories featuring not only the impact of lockdowns and a pandemic but also bushfires, wars, marathons and dystopian futures.

We have a diverse membership and the genres our authors have written in include historical fiction, sci-fi, fantasy, poetry, memoir and literary fiction.

Any book like this requires input from many people; thanks goes to our editor, Kim Smith, for elevating our work with feedback on drafts and proof-reading the final manuscript. Thanks too, to our cover designer, Karen Scott who has made our book look amazing.

None of this would have been possible without the support of the Monash City Libraries and Monash City Council, who sponsor and promote the Writers Group.

Lastly, thank you to the members of the Monash Writers Group. Your hard work and dedication to the project has been inspiring. It was the members who insisted the group be kept running throughout lockdown and maintained our monthly meetings via Zoom while the library was closed.

The group has worked for a year on this project, all the way from the initial decision on theme, to the launch of the completed book. Their feedback when workshopping drafts has made this truly a collective effort.

We hope you enjoy reading this collection as much as we have in putting it together.

Robert New
Chair, Monash Writers Group

Apocalyptic Abyss
Sasha Buntman

Drifting deeply into this dark unknown
Endless thoughts swimming
An insecure fragility
Etched into every vein.

Surreal solitude surrounds us now
In the familiar fields of home
Our sanctuary suddenly
Our entire world.

Uncertainty is our new reality
A compulsory spiritual awakening
What truly matters
And the definition of happiness
Are now a part of everyone's curriculum.

The future holds renewal, transformation, wisdom, faith
and gratitude for all
This dark unknown has beauty too
Glistening gulfs of profound peace
If we let it.

The Unprecedented Times
Mube Akinci-Desem

Norma is walking quickly in the midday heat to the convenience store on the roadside. Her husband and two-year-old daughter are sitting in the car waiting for the cold drinks to quench their thirst. They are on their way to visit the grandparents in Melbourne.

She thinks it's a good thing to have grandparents, her daughter Kyla will enjoy her grandparents' company for a few days. Norma herself cannot remember any of her grandparents. They all passed away by the time she was old enough to remember.

Since there is still quite a distance, they need to stock up on fluids yet again. Carrying the hemp-bag, Norma enters the shop, where the only sound is made by the chime behind the door. A bored-looking middle-aged man is sitting behind the counter. 'G'day. How are you today?'

With a smile plastered on her face, Norma orders. 'Two Coke Zeros, two Sprites, one orange juice and a carton of full-cream milk, please.'

'Travelling far?'

'Going to Melbourne.'

'Where from?'

'Sydney.'

'Have a good trip.'

There is not a single person on the street. Norma perspires by the time she enters the air-conditioned car. Kyla gets her milk first, then Jim gets his favourite Coke Zero and Norma opens her can of Sprite. They continue driving south. Jim says, 'There is another couple of hours to go. I should be alright. Beautiful countryside will keep me awake.'

Norma laughs. 'Well Jim, you didn't let me drive until now. I don't think you'll succumb in the last hour.'

In another hour they stop at a roadside rest area. Kyla and Norma walk to the toilet, then they admire the view of the valley. Jim gets some food out of the esky and they all eat sandwiches. Everyone is in good spirits.

Back on the road Jim asks Norma, 'Can you ring my parents now and tell them we will be there shortly.'

Norma tries and finds there is no response. 'They must be out, Jim.'

'Maybe you can try a little later then?'

Fifteen minutes later Norma tries their home phone, and then her father-in-law's mobile. Still no response. 'They know we are coming today, don't they?'

'Yes, they definitely do.'

They are in suburbia now. Looking around, Norma watches the vista of suburban architecture. There are lots of new buildings coming up. 'Jim, Melbourne is very much like Sydney, isn't it? The rush of development is all around.'

Jim looks around ahead. 'I don't like it when they build so many tiny apartments. So much concrete.'

Norma agrees. 'Yes, the concrete doesn't absorb the heat. We get hotter and hotter.'

Finally, the car pulls up in front of Jim's parents' house. The street is unusually quiet. Norma suddenly thinks, you can drop a pin and hear it. The house is a single-level, detached, brick veneer, with a big garden around it. Norma looks around with renewed interest. The garden is nice and green. Pretty similar to the rest of the street, she reckons.

While Jim is getting Kyla out of her seat, Norma walks up ahead and knocks on the door. No response. Jim and Kyla are walking up to the porch. Kyla is laughing. 'Granpa garden.' Then pointing at the beautiful roses, 'Mummy, Granpa garden.'

Jim has the key; he opens the door and they all enter, making a lot of noise in the large three-bedroom house. Norma notices everything is clean and tidy, but there is nobody around. Jim shouts from the kitchen at the back, 'They must have gone out shopping or something.' 'Have they left any notes, Jim?'

'Can't see any.'

As Jim is carrying the luggage and esky from the car, he stops and looks at the sky. 'It's a beautiful day. Where have they gone?'

Inside, they make themselves comfortable. Norma is getting a drink for Kyla. 'Jim, we haven't seen a single person around. Where are the people in Melbourne?' Jim rings his father's mobile phone again. No response.

Norma checks the fridge. 'There is plenty of food here.' Kyla moves from room to room calling for grandma. 'Jim, why don't you go next door and ask them what they know about your parents' movements.'

'Hey, that's a swell idea, Norma.' He walks out the front door in a hurry.

Jim walks back, looking disappointed. 'I tried both sides. Nobody seems to be home. What do we do?'

Norma is attending to her daughter's grazed knee. Kyla has just had a fall in the backyard. She's crying. 'Oh, there it is. Mummy will kiss it and make it better now.' Eventually Jim picks her up in his arms, cuddling and showing her around the house.

'Kyla, this was my bedroom. Look! I used to keep my toys in this cupboard.' They go and open the cupboard together. 'Ola! Some toys of mine are still here.' Jim looks surprised while Kyla concentrates on the colourful toys. She picks one up and starts moving it slowly. Her father tells Kyla all about the toy truck. 'This one, this yellow truck with big wheels. See. This is how it goes.' Kyla takes it away and pushes it forward herself. Jim goes, 'Vroom. Vrooom.'

Kyla imitates her father. 'Voom. Vooom.'

Norma looks at the time. It's nearly six o'clock. She quickly calculates, Kyla will have to eat and be in bed soon. She calls to Jim, 'Shall we go and do some shopping before we call it a night, Jim?'

'Yes darling. Why not? Let's go.'

Soon they are all in the car heading to the local shopping centre. Jim drives into the car park and finds a parking spot. Norma gets out and shuts her door before she opens the other one to unfasten Kyla. She thinks, it's so weird, it's deadly silent. Apart from the whirring of the air-conditioner.

They start walking towards the automatic doors to enter the mall. Norma is rather frustrated. 'Jim, stop and listen. Can you hear any human sounds?' he does as she bids.

'No darling. It's as if there is nobody here.'

'And yet the car park is full of cars. Isn't that odd?'

They enter and walk around in the centre. The shops are open, but there is nobody around. They are passing a toyshop where Kyla points at something in the window. Jim says, 'Let's go in and have a look. See how much it is.' Inside the toyshop there is a weird silence. There is no shop attendant and nobody to help them. Norma is alarmed.

'Jim, what's wrong with this place? I cannot see a single person anywhere!'

Jim is laughing nervously, 'Maybe there is a big speaking function and they've all gone there. Let's walk around.'

The three of them walk ahead in total silence. Norma can hear their own footsteps echoing. Jim picks up Kyla into his arms and they walk faster to get to the other end of the shopping complex. 'My God! There are no people here.' Norma feels a cold tingling sensation down her back. She holds Jim's arm, tightening her grasp as she tries to make sense of everything around her.

They sit down on a nearby bench quietly. Norma looks directly into Jim's eyes. What she sees in his eyes, she feels inside her. Kyla is sitting in between them, looking from one parent to the other. She is holding her mother's hand really tight. Jim utters, 'Are you thinking what I'm thinking?'

Norma is still as a rock. Not moving a finger. She

hears Jim but cannot respond. Then she says slowly, 'Are you thinking what I'm thinking?'

Norma is now aware that they are the only people in the whole shopping centre. She cannot hide the sense of despair in her voice. 'WHERE ARE THE PEOPLE?' She can hear the sound reverberating again and again.

They stand up and walk in a trance to the car park, get into their car and Jim drives in silence to his parents' house. Norma half expects her in-laws to be back home now. Thinking, willing it all to be a nightmare, she bites her lips, then her tongue, hoping to wake up to reality. It must be blood oozing from her lips, she sees it on her hand. Norma shakes herself and wills her body to sit still, suddenly totally aware of her daughter's presence behind her.

They re-enter the soundless house. Jim walks around, inside the rooms and around the sizeable backyard again and again, calling, 'Mum, Dad. Mother! Father!' He opens the garage and finds their car there in its usual spot. He gets out and walks the length of the street and comes in. Norma is cooking spaghetti. She is feeding her daughter. She is tasting the pasta.

Trying to put some normality to her voice she says, 'Darling, what did you find?'

'Well, lights are turning on at some of the houses. No sign of any people anywhere.'

They sit down to eat. Norma's head is full of stuff. It's racing at the speed of light. She cannot concentrate. Kyla is the only one making any noise, she is banging her hands on the table and making random sounds.

Norma says, 'What about ringing the police? They would have an answer, wouldn't they?' Jim picks up his phone and rings 000. There is no sound, no voice at the other end. 'What happened to these people!' Norma says with a hint of a smile, 'If they are all playing a game of hide and seek, if it's a game, I give up. Please come out now.'

Jim tries the TV. There is erratic noises and shapes. They go to bed after a while. Just before he doses off, Jim says, 'Tomorrow we need to read the newspapers.'

Norma laughs bitterly. 'If there is no delivery, how are we to get hold of them, Jim?'

Next morning, when Norma wakes up with swollen eyes, she finds Jim and Kyla playing with toys. She runs out to the backyard and has a good cry before coming in to get breakfast ready.

After breakfast Jim says, 'Let's all go for a long drive. See what's happening further afield.'

Norma agrees. 'Yes, let's do that at least. But,' she slows down, 'but before that why don't you ring Roger in Sydney. You know, your friend.'

He stops in his tracks. 'Yeah. Why don't I do that.'

Quickly he rings Roger. The ringtone is incessant. Jim is about to give up when Roger can be heard, 'Hello, who's there?'

Norma is visibly weeping from the pleasant surprise of finding someone, anyone, alive somewhere.

She could hear Jim talking to someone. When he turns the phone off Jim looks more confused than before. 'Darling, nobody seems to know what happened.'

Norma tries to get Jim to calm down. 'Now Jim. Tell me exactly what he said. Please.'

Jim is looking at her with eyes almost coming out of their sockets. He says, 'Well, Roger doesn't know either.

He said there was a lot of talk about aliens. Some people are saying the Chinese have bombed Melbourne. Some think it's a joke. Everyone in Sydney is shocked.'

'What about the government in Canberra? What are they saying?'

'Roger doesn't know. He said there is also a lot of talk of viral warfare. How could so many millions disappear without a trace?' Frustrated he says, 'Let's go for a drive then.'

They pile into the car and drive along a major highways. Norma notices, 'Not a car is going by anywhere.'

Jim adds, 'And not a person is walking anywhere.'

They drive south, they drive north, they drive west. It's the same everywhere. Jim says, 'Petrol is low.'

As he is driving into a petrol station Norma says, 'Can you fill up just like that?'

Shrugging his shoulders, Jim gets out and fills the tank. He walks in to pay and returns in a hurry. 'Norma! What shall I do? Should I leave the cash on the counter?' Almost to himself, 'Who will pick it up?'

Norma is lost in thought herself. She is beckoning for him to come inside. Jim is confused, 'So, I don't pay?' He reluctantly sits down in the driver's seat and shuts the door. They sit there for aeons, not doing anything at all.

Norma comes out of her inner coma, becomes aware of her surroundings a little at a time. She thinks, why is Jim sitting there? What did he just say to me? Why is he not moving? Where are the people? She's pinching herself to make sure she is not dreaming. 'Is this a nightmare? Jim, where are we going now?' Jim starts the car. Norma notices Jim looks as determined as a log.

He is out of the petrol station, slowly driving on the road. They see a man running towards them. Jim stops the car. He looks at Norma, as if asking what to do. The man comes closer and starts banging on the car window to open. Norma sees a demented look on the man's face. She quietly says, 'Is it safe to open the window?' The man is pleading with them to open. Norma notices a large shallow wound on his neck, with dried blood covering the left side. She concludes there is nothing she can do to help. The pus is dry. Strangely enough, her training as a nurse has not prepared her for this. She looks across at Jim, who normally is the calmest person she knows. Jim's face is contorted as he looks straight ahead, with his foot on the brake and his hands gripping the steering wheel.

The man stops banging, he is presumably watching them quietly. Norma has eye contact with the injured man for a fleeting second. She sees a madman begging for mercy with his whole being. His face is black and blue. His once white shirt is torn in several places.

Norma imagines he murdered another man, was himself injured during the fight. She imagines it was over some precious thing they couldn't share amicably. In the current situation, people can get away with murder. Norma imagines the man came from a country town, perhaps he lost his whole family. She notices Jim is driving away from the man.

They keep driving for a while. Nobody says anything. Even Kyla is very quiet. Eventually Norma cannot take the suspense. 'Jim, why did we leave the injured man behind? And where are we going?'

There is no immediate response. Then, 'Norma, I don't know what I'm doing. What shall we do?' comes a feeble reply.

Norma feels her head is cloudy. She whispers, 'I'm confused too, Jim.'

She then tries to rise to the occasion. 'I think we have two options; drive back to Sydney or go back and help that injured man.' She adds, 'Not that I can help him or his wound much.'

Jim looks at her with intense surprise. 'What! Go back and help that madman! Are you out of your mind? What if he attacks us?'

For a few seconds there is total silence again. Norma is thinking about Kyla now. If something happened to them, Kyla would be left alone in the lifeless wilderness of Melbourne. No! They cannot go back, obviously.

They are driving to Jim's parents' place. Soon the journey is broken by a woman rushing towards them, waving her arms wildly. Norma's immediate reaction is, we don't have to worry about being attacked. She turns to look at her husband and he is looking at her with concentration. 'What do we do, Norma?'

Norma finds herself outside the car talking to this mature-age woman who seems like a practical person. Her name is Fiona and she speaks very fast. 'I have been walking for the last couple of hours. There's nobody at home. Nobody on the streets. There's nobody anywhere.'

Norma asks, 'When did you realise there was nobody around?'

She thinks for a moment as if rewiring her brain. 'I know! I went into the cellar to choose a bottle of wine. We were expecting visitors in the evening, you see. I think I was under the house for maybe twenty minutes.' She starts to cry and stutter a little. 'When I came out of the cellar, I couldn't find John, my husband, anywhere in the house.' She is having difficulty putting her thoughts together. 'I … I … I thought he'd gone out somewhere. A bit unusual, but. I tidied up and then cleaned the kitchen. Then I went sh … sh … shopping. Th … there was not a person in the sh … sh … shopping centre. I got really scared. Wh … what happened? Do you know?'

Norma doesn't know what to say. 'We are from Sydney. When did this whole thing happen?'

The woman stops and thinks, 'Well, I haven't seen my husband for two days. So, whatever this is, it happened two nights ago.'

'What do you think happened to your husband, Fiona?' Norma is very gentle. 'Have you noticed anything missing at home? Like, did John disappear with just the clothes on his back?'

Fiona is thinking back to two nights ago. 'Yes. He magically vanished. Just like that. Nothing else is missing.'

Norma tells her about her in-laws. She also tells her about the shopping centre with no people in it, but where the car park is full of cars. They hug and hug again silently. Norma is now thinking about this woman and what her needs might be. What can they do? Jim and Norma look at each other, totally puzzled.

As they are driving away from Fiona, a little while later, Norma looks back through the rear-view mirror. Fiona is standing there, rooted like an ancient tree with no leaves, tears running down her face, about to question the meaning of existence.

Norma's eyes are moist, as she makes a heartfelt despairing statement into the air, 'Unprecedented times! Yes. Unprecedented times!'

An Unfortunate Side Effect of War

Ingrid Fry

Ancient brown photographs; a family portrait, people standing stiff and upright, reminding me of store mannequins. Only the eyes seem lifelike: Huge liquid brown eyes gazing at me from the past.

My mind strains to capture the memories of childhood. My father, such fleeting, melancholy memories. So tall and handsome in the photographs; I remember you as being kindly. It's strange that most of the knowledge I have is second hand.

A forester in Austria, his uniform was coloured with forest greens. His work was a great joy to him, as he loved being close to nature. He planted seedlings, cared for the forests, and occasionally shot stags when they became too numerous.

I was not yet born when the First World War began, and my father had to leave his work to go and fight.

As most of the fighting was carried out on foot or horseback, the Russians sought ways to increase their firepower. Often, if there were rock formations close by, the Russians would place explosives underneath them, their detonation sending fragments of rock hurtling at the enemy.

My father was hit by one of these flying rocks. The impact was so great it spun him around on his feet like a top. He collapsed, and although his left arm was torn away at the shoulder, he remained fully conscious throughout the trip to the hospital.

I look again in disbelief at the tiny sepia coloured photograph taken at the hospital. The stuff of nightmares. It is dark and indistinct, but I can see my father's head wrapped in bandages, and his arm – supported by the doctor – hanging off his shoulder, attached only by a strip of tendon.

His arm was amputated, and eventually he was returned home. As a result of his injury he could no longer work as a forester, so he was given employment as an office clerk.

My father's arm refused to heal properly and gave him much trouble. Even after three years, his arm was still weeping and causing pain. The doctors had tried everything, so eventually he was sent to have blood tests. The results were devastating; he was diagnosed as having syphilis.

Three years prior, at the field hospital, when receiving the initial treatment on his arm, he had been given a blood transfusion. The blood was from a syphilitic man.

No outward physical signs appeared to warn him because of the direct infection into the bloodstream. By the time the disease was discovered, a cure was virtually impossible.

His health slowly declined. His muscular and nervous systems were affected, causing him to stagger and lose control of his bodily functions. His brain deteriorated, bringing memory loss and emotional outbursts. He often became lost, and neighbours would find him and bring him home. The disease was slow in its effect. He would spend weeks at a time in hospital where the doctors would infect him with malaria in the hope that the fever would destroy the syphilis. When my mother took me to visit, the doctors would bring my father out in a straitjacket, as the fever would make him violent.

My sister and I had to have blood tests too, for it was feared we may also be infected. Luckily, the results were negative.

Soon it became too much for my mother to bear, as she had to clean and care for my father as if he were a child. In 1938, shortly after Hitler invaded Austria, he was hospitalised permanently in a home for the mentally disabled. At that time, telephones were scarce, so the hospital asked for the number of a local shop – the bakery - which could pass on a message to our family if father's condition became critical.

It was a Thursday when Mum and I walked the many miles to the hospital to see him. It was a cold, windy day and I can still visualise the huge banners emblazoned with the swastika, fluttering from buildings and churches.

We took my father coffee and fresh donuts, which he loved. He had times when he was completely lucid and happy, and this was such a day. Our return home was laughter-filled, my mother joyous with the notion of his recovery.

Two small rooms were our home at that time. Poverty

was our neighbour, but despite the difficult conditions, our surroundings were kept neat and clean, flowers always on the table. In the mornings, the baker would call and hang a string bag full of freshly baked bread rolls on the door handle.

On the Monday morning after we had been to the hospital, the baker popped in. He came to offer his condolences.

The look of bewilderment that rushed over my mother's face is still with me. I see her faded floral apron, darned stockings, wrinkled brow, and frightened eyes. I hear her voice; sharp, taut with anxiety, questioning.

'There must be some mistake!'

'Oh, I am so sorry,' the baker said, his eyes filling with tears. 'They must have forgotten to pass on the message. Your husband passed away suddenly on Saturday morning.'

Frightened and chilled by the howls of anguish that issued from my mother, I wondered whether she was dying or injured in some way. I hear her words muttered over and over again, '… but he looked so well, he looked so well …'

My father was buried the following day, along with all the other patients from the hospital. It seemed that everyone had passed away on that Saturday morning.

My father died twenty-two years after his injury. Our family received neither pension nor compensation because the government decreed he had not died of a war injury.

Azaleas in Springtime

Sakuntala Gananathan

Would you believe me if I declare that long before Covid-19 impacted people's social interaction, we maintained a pseudo social distancing in the neighbourhood? Don't think me daft. It's absolutely true. Most of the residents have occupied the same houses for the past fifteen, twenty years, but each family lived in a cocoon. We hardly made an effort to get to know one another. At the most we might have exchanged a smile or nod while out on a walk.

This state of affairs continued until Tracey Johnstone, a single woman in her sixties, moved into the cottage next door. She was like a breath of fresh air on a sultry afternoon. It was as though the handsome prince had kissed Sleeping Beauty, after which all of us were awakened from an enchanted sleep.

From then on there was nothing to stop us from socialising with one another. We were lending books, sharing jokes and anecdotes, and partaking in house parties. At Christmas, Santa came door knocking with goodies. Santa invariably was Tracey, her silver hair giving away the secret, much to the delight of the kids. Our daughter would cook large quantities of biriyani, naan, rotti and butter chicken, and invite neighbours to join us in Diwali celebrations.

In late winter and early springtime, Tracey's potted azaleas were a mix of vibrant hues. She wouldn't fail to hand out cuttings on our birthdays and encouraged us to grow them in our gardens. Come October, and it is Halloween. She would join the young and old to go trick-or-treating.

~

As though heralding the unprecedented time that was soon to impact us, in February of this year Tracey suffered a severe chest pain, but she had the presence of mind to press on the vital call pendant. Within minutes an ambulance was there to take her to hospital. We were thoroughly distressed.

After she was transferred from the ICU, I paid her a visit in the hospital. She whispered with much difficulty, 'I've asked the PO to direct my mails to my lawyers.'

A nurse hurried over and propped her up with pillows, after which she was able to speak better. 'After I am discharged from Rehab, I have decided to move into a residential aged-care home.'

Although taken aback, I was careful not to show my shock and unhappiness. 'I do welcome your decision, Tracey, but I am going to miss you very much, dear.'

'That makes two of us.'

As I prepared to leave, she beckoned me to come closer. 'I wish to gift my potted azaleas to my nephew, Michael. He would call you before he collects them.'

'I shall pass the word around, so that he is not accused of housebreaking!'

Kids down the road took upon themselves to lawn mow Tracey's garden and water her plants. Thereafter, they were hired by some of the other residents. As unanimously agreed by the youngsters, monies paid to them in return for services rendered, are to be donated to The Smith Family Charity supporting disadvantaged Australian kids.

A letter purported to have been sent me by my accountant seemed to have gone astray. I lodged a complaint at our post office that a particular letter of importance was not delivered to me. One of their staff made a thorough search, while I admired the man's long brown hair tied up with a golden ribbon. The queue behind me was getting restless and someone coughed to gain his attention. So, he shook his head and said, 'I would suggest you peep into your immediate neighbour's letter box. I bet it's there!'

By Jove the letter was there in Tracey's letter box! It was damp and crushed underneath junk mail, and gaped at me like a long-lost orphan!!

~

Tracey's only daughter Jennifer was settled down in Birmingham, UK. I have had the pleasure of meeting her whenever she came over to visit her mother. She called me in mid-July to convey the sad news that her mum had passed away the previous week. She said that because of Covid-19 travel restrictions, she was unable to come over, but had partaken in her mother's funeral service on Zoom. She added that she had instructed the lawyers to keep the house closed until such time as she was able to travel Down Under.

All of us were heartbroken. To add to our grief, Tracey's passing away coincided with the spurt of Coronavirus casualties in Victoria. No more sharing books or plates of sweets and savouries. We have a quick chat with others across their fences, and are home well before 8pm.

Seems like we have retreated into our scabbards as in the pre-Tracey era. Yet, there is a difference. Earlier it was a self-styled social distancing in our neighbourhood. Now it is coupled with strict physical distancing of at least six feet from one another. Wearing face masks is mandatory. For Metropolitan Melbourne, curfews are in place from 8:00pm to 5:00am to reduce the number of people leaving their homes and moving around.

~

While we were having dinner a fortnight ago, a car screeched to a sudden halt outside our gate, followed by a piercing police siren. I pushed my plate away and awaited with nervous tension for the doorbell to ring. Nothing happened. Long past midnight I sneaked downstairs to the kitchen and raided the refrigerator to have a snack and a cup of milk, after which I was able to sleep peacefully.

As was customary in our neighbourhood, none bothered to ascertain the reason for the commotion that night. We went about our business the next day and the day after. On the third day, I came across Bertram, walking with his shoulders hunched. He seemed to have aged of a sudden. He and his family live in the house directly opposite ours. I inquired after his health.

Without much fanfare he said, 'My daughter Sylvia

was slapped a heavy fine for breaching curfew hours. I paid the money and assured the officer it wouldn't happen again.'

'I'm sorry to hear of it, Bertram.' Although I didn't voice my fears, he seemed to have guessed what was in my mind.

'Lucky she reached home without serious mishap. I have hidden her car keys after the fiasco! Kenneth and she were having dinner and didn't realise it was nearing 8pm. He had a pass to show the officer who let him off. Sylvia made her exit through the rear entrance and made a dash home, with police trailing her.'

'Lucky Cinderella!' Sylvia called out as she jogged past us. 'She was given four more hours to get home!'

~

Since the introduction of the pandemic restrictions, I have started making a few phone calls to friends and relatives, especially older folks living in isolation at home or living in aged-care homes in Australia and abroad. I play some music for them to listen, or relate a funny story to cheer them up. While patiently hearing their chatter, which invariably would be repetition of jokes and previous conversations, at appropriate moments I interrupt them to ask, 'Is that so?' or 'What happened next?'

We have weekly Zoom meetings with friends and relatives here in Australia and abroad, at a convenient time for all of us.

Our grandkids are following online school sessions with mixed feelings. Some of them prefer direct interaction with their teachers. They miss playing netball and football at the weekends. In order to humour them, we play board games whenever they are free. They have turned out to be good cooks in the past few months, and help their mothers with the vegetable patch in their backyards. They seldom listen to news channels, and are happy to get sports updates from their mobile phones. All of them are anxious to get to school and they hope matters would soon return to normal.

My daughters are working from home, and do their grocery shopping on Saturdays. On Sundays they stitch cloth face masks to distribute to neighbours and friends.

~

Last Saturday the kids wished to have mee goreng and fish buns for lunch. I picked a bag full of ripe lemons from our backyard and set off in a hurry.

'Hi!' called out Marianne, Bertram's wife. She was unloading her shopping from the car boot. 'Where are you rushing to?'

'To get mee goreng and fish buns.'

'But you could have asked your daughter to buy them for you. She is still there at Coles. Why not give her a call?'

'I'm taking a walk to the corner shop, run by a couple known to us. They are struggling to survive. Competition is tough, they say. Their son has been laid off and it adds to their woes. I was told that they would need a minimum of $5,500 per month to pay for the rent and to get food at their table.'

At the corner shop I dropped the lemons into an empty box beside the owner's wife.

'Thank you, dear.'

While I was paying for the purchases, I happened to notice a large laundry basket, laden with books and what not. It was the same basket I had seen a fortnight earlier.

It was painted shocking pink and had sky blue ribbons tied around it. During the time of hard waste collection, there were heaps of stuff thrown out on grass patches alongside the road. They were of little value or of no value, or things that were irreparable. One morning I saw Elissa Yousuf, who lives at No. 16, drag the basket lying among hard waste further down our road. *With a baby on the way, she would need the basket perhaps,* I had thought at the time.

The shop owner gave me the balance money and noticed me staring at the basket. 'A young woman presented us with that basket. It has come of great use to us.'

Walking back home, I was still thinking of the donor of the basket, and great was my surprise to see Elissa herself. She crossed over and fell into step with me. We made sure to keep a safe distance between us.

'I thanked your daughter for giving me a book titled, *What to Expect when you are Expecting.* I am very happy we have come to this country. Everybody is helpful and understanding. But this sense of anxiety is always troubling me. Yousuf has nicknamed me Elissa Worrier! We hope and pray things return to normal before I have my baby.'

'Why not listen to some light music to lift your spirits. Or watch a comedy show. That's how some of us entertain ourselves at home in order to break the monotony.'

'What if I develop pains when Yousuf is at work? He is on duty three nights a week.'

I did my best to distract her with some funny anecdotes my husband comes up with whenever I feel out of sorts. Alas! It was of no use.

'I am reminded of my countryman's poem. Have you ever heard of Kahlil Gibran?' she asked.

'Certainly yes. I believe he had settled down in the US and died when he was in his forties.'

'Take a listen while I quote a few lines from one of his poems titled FEAR.'

'Elissa, please don't. I would rather we discuss something light; something that would make us happy in this unprecedented time.'

She was, however, in a world of her own. Rolling her eyes, she began reciting the poem as though she were on stage, addressing a large gathering:

"It is said that before entering the sea
a river trembles with fear
She looks at the path she has travelled,
from the peaks of the mountains,
the long winding road crossing forests and villages.
And in front of her
she sees an ocean so vast
that to enter
there seems nothing more than to disappear forever…"

'Would you shut up, Elissa!' Even as the words escaped my mouth, I felt thoroughly ashamed of myself. What right have I to impose my views upon her? A young mother to be?

Shocked and annoyed with me, she increased her pace.

I called out, 'Would you please forgive me for my outburst!' As I tried to hold back my tears, one of my

24

parcels slipped from my hands.

It took a while for Elissa to cool down. She stopped walking and turned to me. 'You are panting. Let me carry one of your parcels.'

'Thank you, no.' I quickly picked the parcel up before she could reach for it.

A heavy silence fell between us. As we neared her home, I said, 'It's springtime now. Azaleas are in full bloom in our gardens. We need to thank good old Tracey for them. Bless her soul.'

Despite the mask she had on, I could see Elissa's face muscles soften. 'Bless her soul,' she repeated.

'My dear Elissa, it's best we meditate upon positive matters during this unprecedented time. When you are alone at home, especially while Yousuf is at work, why not spend a little time with your unborn baby?'

She was thoughtful for a few minutes, while I looked on anxiously. She placed her hands softly on her tummy and murmured, 'Yes, why not I sing to my unborn baby?'

~

After the continuous gale and rain that lashed most parts of Victoria the last couple of days, my husband and I were able to take a walk this morning.

Yousuf stopped washing his car and came over to speak to us. He hitched on his face mask and whispered, 'I'm catching up on lost sleep these days. Your fairy dust is working! Thank you!!'

Turbulent Times in Isolation
Ruth Kweitel

'Em, it's almost lunchtime; time to get up,' Jessica called out to her daughter.

'OK Mum, I'll get up soon,' she replied, as tears began streaming down her face. She rolled over and buried her face in her pillow, unaware that her mother was watching her from her bedroom door, which was slightly ajar.

'Emily,' Jessica repeated. On hearing her mother's voice, Emily turned to face her.

'Darling, what on earth's the matter? Why are you so upset?' Jessica asked, as she sat herself on the bed next to Emily and began pushing Emily's damp blond hair back from her daughter's tear-stained face.

'Mum, I hate uni and I hate my subjects. I haven't made any friends yet and now we're all in lockdown and I can't make any. I've hardly had a chance to settle in and now I'm stuck at home. To make matters worse, my school friends have forgotten I exist. I haven't heard from any of them. They're probably having a great time. I'm the only one that didn't get into my first choice for uni and I don't like what I've got.' Tears began to pour down Emily's face as her body convulsed with sobs. 'To top things off, I've also lost my job, thanks to the pandemic, and that was the only thing that kept me sane. I got the sack yesterday. Now give me a good reason why I should get out of bed?' Emily turned away from her mother to face the wall and continued to sob.

'Darling, I don't want to talk to your back so please turn around to face me. Why didn't you tell me you lost your job?'

'I didn't want to worry you. You've had a hard time since Dad passed away and I didn't want to burden you with more stuff.'

'Em, you're making lots of assumptions about me and your school friends and, without any firsthand knowledge. Firstly, stop worrying about me. I'm managing quite well on my own and just because schools have closed, doesn't mean my job's gone. I'm teaching from home. It's a new experience for me but at least my job isn't at risk. I've still got an income. Secondly, you really don't know how your school friends are coping because you haven't been in touch with them since uni started. None of you have been at uni long enough to find your feet and the pandemic has now become a huge disruption for everyone, especially since we're all in lockdown. People who can work from home have to and all students including school kids, will be doing their subjects online so just because you haven't had any contact with your school friends, doesn't mean they're OK. Everyone has lots of adjustments to make, whether we like it or not. Uni is nothing like high school and doing your studies online is very different to a classroom and even a lecture theatre. Teaching from home is also different to a classroom so we both have to make some adjustments to our lives, as does everybody. These times are unprecedented so we're all treading in unchartered waters. Stop feeling sorry for yourself and get out of bed. You'd better get used to this way of life because the isolation isn't going to finish tomorrow, nor the next day or the day after that. Why don't you take the first step and phone Mandy? You were besties at school and you've been good friends for years. Good friendships don't disappear overnight. Maybe Mandy hasn't phoned you because she's also struggling with all the changes that have been imposed. Life's difficult for everyone at the moment.'

'Yeah, alright, I'll call her but it doesn't change the fact that I'm really pissed off about my job. I like working more than uni. I think I should've taken a gap year. I need breathing space and besides, I love getting wages every week.'

'Em, your job loss is the least of your worries. You have a roof over your head and food on the table. The store closures are time limited. They will eventually reopen and hopefully you'll get your job back. While we have social isolation and lockdown, you don't need any money because you won't be going anywhere. Your problems are nothing compared to what other people are going through. Now get off your bum and call Mandy and stop thinking about yourself for a change. There are stacks of people who can't pay their rent, let alone have money for food or even run a car, and they have kids to support.'

'OK, OK I get the message,' Emily replied huffily. *Just*

what I need now, one of Mum's lectures while I feel like shit. Emily watched her mother exit her bedroom. As soon as she was out of sight, Emily grabbed her mobile phone and checked her messages; still nothing from Mandy. *Bitch. I'll bet she's having a great time*. Emily then got up, donned her jogging gear which lay crumpled on the floor, filled her water bottle and grabbed her phone

'Mum, I'm going for a jog. I'll call Mandy when I get back.'

'OK but remember the restrictions. Only go for a short time, no detours en route and comply with social distancing.'

'Yeah, OK. I'll be back when you see me. You worry too much and stop treating me like a little kid,' Emily replied, as she grabbed her keys.

'When you get back, I'll be taking a class online, so please no noise. If you ring Mandy later, maybe do it in the backyard. I don't want my class distracted by what you're doing in the background.'

Emily left and as soon as she got out the gate, she began to run in the direction of the park a couple of streets away. It only took her a few minutes to get there. She stopped suddenly at the entrance. *Wow, the park's almost empty. Great, I can run without any disruptions and distractions*. Emily entered the park and ran in the direction of the lake. She turned her music up loud and jogged to the rhythm of the music. *This is so nice and peaceful. I don't need to talk to anyone. I can just listen to the music and enjoy the environmen*t. After a few laps around the lake, Emily felt better so decided to sit down on one of the seats and phone Amanda. Just as she took her mobile from its case, a young man sat down on the same seat beside her.

'G'day,' Lachlan greeted Emily with a big smile. 'Do you exercise in this park often?' he asked.

'No, not really. I'm here because of lockdown. Exercising here gives me a legit reason to get away from home and my mother. This lockdown shit is unbelievable. I'd normally be at uni which I hate and now I've got no job so I come here for a bit of peace. How about you?'

'I have to work from home so I occasionally come to the park for some fresh air. By the way, what's your name?'

'I'm Emily but everyone calls me Em. What's yours?'

'I'm Lachlan but everyone calls me Lachie.'

'I figured that. I've never seen you here before. Do you come here often?'

'No, not really. I normally work in an office with other people in a large space. Now that I'm working from home, I feel a bit cooped up and lonely at times. When that happens, I come here to clear my head. I mainly come weekdays, to break up my working day a little bit.' Lachie looked at his watch. 'Jeez, I've got to get going. I have a Zoom meeting soon. This was short and sweet. I'll leave you to your jogging. Maybe we'll catch up again soon, cheers.' Lachie stood up and quickly made his way to the park exit. As Emily watched him go she started to think about him and couldn't believe her luck. *Wow, he's such a cool guy, tall, good-looking and he's so nice. Wait till Mandy hears about this.*

As soon as Lachie was out of sight, Emily rang Mandy's mobile. When the voicemail clicked in, she hung up. *That's weird. It's not like Mandy not to answer her phone.* Emily stood up and continued to jog around the lake. After an hour had passed, she decided to go home. As soon as she got there, before she went inside, Emily decided to call Mandy again. After a couple of rings, Mandy's mother answered the phone.

'Hi Emily, it's Dianne, Mandy's mother.'

'Oh, hi Dianne, I wasn't expecting you to answer the phone. Can I please speak to Mandy?'

'Sorry Emily, she can't take calls at the moment; she's very unwell.'

'Really, has she got Covid-19?' Emily jumped in.

'No, no, nothing like that. Her Covid test was negative. The doctor thinks she may have glandular fever. We're waiting for test results.'

'That's awful. Are you sure it's not Covid? There's a lot of stuff on Facebook saying the tests aren't accurate. Some people are saying there are false positives and false negatives. Sometimes it's hard to know what to believe.'

'No, we're very sure it's not that. When she's feeling better I'll let her know you called and she'll call you back. It may be a couple of weeks before she gets back to you. She's pretty tired much of the day. Take care and stay safe. Bye for now.' Mandy's mother hung up before Emily could respond.

She then went inside and went straight to her room, so as not to disturb her mother. She lay down on the bed, closed her eyes and tried to visualise Lachie. *I wonder how old he is. This lockdown may not be so bad after all.* Emily suddenly felt much happier. She jumped off the bed, went and showered, opened up her computer and started to catch up with the online lectures she'd neglected and had fallen behind with. She became so engrossed with her lectures she jumped at the knock on her door.

'Come on in Mum,' Emily called out.

'How was your jog? Many people in the park?'

'Nuh, it was great. Nice and peaceful. It cleared my head a lot," Emily replied, smiling at her mother.

'That's good to hear. Em darling, this morning you were very upset, moping and teary and now you seem to have made a rather quick recovery. How come? Mind you, I'm not complaining. Anything I need to know?'

"Nuh. Not really. The jog in the park made a big difference. I can feel when the endorphins kick in and that makes me feel better. I've decided to jog every day. It'll help keep me fit and motivated even if I hate the isolation. By the way, I rang Mandy. She's sick. Her mother answered her phone. They think she's got glandular.'

'I'm sorry to hear that. She'll be infectious so you won't be able to visit for a while. See, I told you there'd be a good reason why Mandy hadn't called.'

For god's sake, shut up Mum, Emily thought as she rolled her eyes just long enough for Jessica to notice.

'Emily, would you mind not rolling your eyes at me when I'm speaking to you.'

'Sorry Mum, I need to catch up on my lectures and then I've also got assignments to think about. I've been so tired I've got a bit behind lately, in fact, I'm a lot behind. Please close the door on your way out.'

'OK Em, I get the message,' Jessica replied as she exited the room with a half - smile on her face. *Thank goodness she seems to have recovered from her misery this morning,* Jessica thought.

The next day Emily got up bright and cheerful, as though yesterday hadn't happened. She looked at her grotty active wear lying crumpled on the floor. She picked up her t-shirt, took a sniff and immediately dropped it as she screwed up her nose. Emily wondered if she would see Lachie again. She gave herself a light spray of Opium and donned her new active wear that had been sitting in her drawer since Christmas. Emily smiled as she checked herself out in the mirror. *For once, Mum's got pretty cool taste in sportswear.* Jessica noticed Em was finally wearing her new clothes and was pleased and relieved at the change in her daughter. Now she felt she could fully focus on her job. Just before she was about to connect onto Zoom, Emily interrupted her.

'Mum, I'm going to continue jogging to the park and around the lake every day. What I thought I'd do is take a sandwich with me and have my lunch there as well so I'll be gone a bit longer than usual.'

'I don't think taking lunch is a good idea. You're only supposed to be out for exercise. Remember the restrictions.'

'Yeah, I know, but each time I've gone to the park, there's hardly anyone there. No-one will see me. Sometimes I'm the only one. If someone sees me and I get challenged, I'll say I'm a diabetic and that I have to eat immediately after my run.'

'Em, that's lying and taking a risk and, I don't like it. It's wrong and it's against the law. What's the matter with you? I never thought you'd be one of those stupid and reckless people who would challenge restrictions.'

'God Mum, I'm not going to breathe germs over anyone and this isolation shit is getting to me. This is the only way I can cope otherwise I'll end up staying in bed all day. I struggle getting up every morning because I'm constantly tired. I'm behind with my uni stuff and I hate my life at the moment.' Jessica passed her daughter a tissue when she saw tears begin to well up in Emily's eyes.

'Darling, I hear what you're saying however, just because you aren't on campus doesn't mean uni doesn't exist and I can't afford to pay any fine if you get caught breaching restrictions. We're in a pandemic. I know you are upset about a few things and you've got good reason to be. However, my concern for you is that you may becoming a bit depressed. Your behaviour is beginning to worry me. You're starting to remind me of your father.'

'Mum you're so overprotective, I'm fine. You're smothering me. I know Dad was depressed. I'm not. I just need an outing so I'm going to take my lunch to the park. The quiet and the fresh air calms me down and jogging improves my motivation.'

'OK it's up to you, if it makes you feel better however, but I am concerned about your weepiness.'

'Mu–um, please.'

'OK OK but, I expect you to comply with the restrictions so if there's anyone in the park, you do the social distancing and bring your lunch back and eat it at home. Don't take any risks. Can I trust you to do that?'

'Since when have you not been able to trust me?'

'Since a few minutes ago when you told me about your sneaky plan to eat in the park.'

'Don't worry. Everything'll be fine.'

Emily made herself a sandwich, filled her water bottle, grabbed her mobile, an apple from the fridge and put everything in her backpack. She then made her way to the park. As soon as she got to the entrance, she looked around. No-one in sight. *I wonder if Lachie will come,* she thought, as she made her way to the same seat where they met. She took out her sandwich and, just as she took her first bite, she felt a tap on the back of her shoulder. Emily's body jerked, causing her to drop her sandwich.

'G'day Em. Oh crap, I've made you drop your sandwich. Did I scare you coming up from behind? Sorry about that,' he said with a big grin on his face.

"Nah. I'm OK. I was just lost in my own thoughts and wasn't expecting to see you or anyone,' she lied.

'Mind if I sit down. I now owe you a lunch.'

'Sure, take a seat. Don't worry about the sandwich. I'm supposed to be dieting anyway but I'll hold you to a lunch when this pandemic shit is over. I don't know about you, but this isolation is really getting to me.'

'Yeah but it is what it is and, there's nothing we can do except suck it up. No point getting angry about it. It's out of our control. Did you say you're on a diet? A gorgeous babe like you?' Emily began to rummage in her backpack, pretending to search for something while trying to hide her face as it got hotter and a flush began to rise from her neck and up into her cheeks

'Lachie, we're going to have to be careful sitting here. I'm not supposed to be eating lunch and we're supposed to be social distancing, not socialising.'

'Don't worry Em, if the cops come sniffing around, I'll do the talking.'

'Oh, I don't know if that's such a good idea. Are you sure?'

'Chill out Em. I've never seen anyone here monitoring social distancing and I've been coming here every day for the last week. Now, if I remember rightly, yesterday you told me you'd lost your job. Are you interested in getting another one?'

'Yeah. Do you know of a job going?'

'Yes I do but it's full time and you told me you go to uni.'

'Stuff uni, I'd love a full-time job. I should've deferred this year and didn't. Now I'm sorry.'

'What about your mother? She won't want you to leave uni.'

'Lachie, leave her to me. I'll tell her when it suits me. In the meantime, I'll continue with my uni stuff, so she won't suspect anything.'

'OK, I'll send you the details of the job and an application. If you're successful, you'll be put on a 3-month trial. You'll be assessed as to how quickly you adapt to the job and pick up the required skills. If you do well and you impress HR, they'll offer you an ongoing position at the end of the three months. OK, now that we've got the job and your mother sorted, give me your contact details,' Lachie asked, as he handed Emily his mobile. She entered her details without a second thought, then handed back the phone.

'Give me a couple of days to get in touch with my contacts. You'll probably be notified in a couple of weeks.'

'Lachie, I can't believe it. Thank you soooo much. Yay, farewell uni,' an excited Emily exclaimed

'Lachie, this is the best thing that's happened to me in a long time. Can I give you a hug?' Emily asked.

Lachie stood up and eyed off Emily. 'What about social distancing,' he said as he began to smirk.

'Fuck that Lachie,' Em blurted out as she jumped up and rushed in, closely hugging him. Lachie began to laugh as he quickly pulled her arms from around his neck.

'I have to get going Em. Enjoy what's left of your lunch. Stay safe. Will I see you tomorrow?'

'Yep, I'll be here, same time, same place.'

'Great. Don't forget I owe you a lunch. See you tomorrow.'

Emily watched Lachie leave while she slowly finished her lunch. As she walked home, she couldn't stop thinking about him. *Oh my god, what a guy. He's so cool and much more mature than those dudes at uni.*

'How was your lunch in the park?' Jessica asked, as Emily walked in the door.

'Well, I dropped one half of my sandwich, so I chucked it out. I ate the rest but wasn't really hungry. My appetite seems to have disappeared. Don't know why. Jogging usually makes me hungry. Not today.'

'Are you feeling OK? You seem to be more tired than usual and you're really moody. You seem so different to your usual self.'

'Mum, I've told you before, please stop worrying about me. I'll tell you if there's a problem,' Emily replied

'I'm going to my room to check my emails and then do some uni work. I can't believe how far behind I am.'

'I'm relieved your motivation has returned. I don't think you realise that without a degree or profession, you won't be able to get a decent job.'

'I know all that Mum, you've told me at least ten times,' Emily said as she rolled her eyes.

'Em, enough with the eye rolling. It's becoming a bad habit of yours and I don't like it. You need to show me a bit more respect and if you did, you wouldn't be apologising to me every five minutes either.'

'Sorry Mum. I'm going to my room. I jogged hard

today and I feel a bit knocked out. I have a lecture on Zoom at 4 o'clock. Can you please wake me if I sleep through the alarm?'

'Em, you need to take more responsibility for yourself.'

Here we go again, another mini-lecture, Emily thought as she wandered into her bedroom. As soon as she got close enough to the bed, she threw herself onto it. *I'm so knackered, I don't think I can sit up to take my shoes off*, she thought as her heavy eyelids closed and she drifted into a deep sleep.

Emily's alarm rang at 4pm. The sound continued to ring for what seemed like an eternity. Jessica rushed into Emily's bedroom and turned off the alarm.

'Em, Em its 4 o'clock," Jessica pleaded while shaking her daughter, trying to get her to wake up

'Mum, I'm so tired, I can't do the lecture, I need more sleep.' As Emily turned around, Jessica gasped at the sight of Emily's flushed face and immediately put the back of her hand on Emily's forehead.

'Em, your cheeks are bright red and your skin feels hot. How do you feel?'

'Mum, leave me alone. I'm tired, I can hardly wake up and my throat's a bit sore.' Jessica left Emily and returned with a thermometer to take her temperature.

'Darling you have a fever. I think you should have a Covid test.'

'I'm so tired. We'll go tomorrow. By then, I'll be much better. I wore myself out jogging.'

'Em, I'm contacting Dr Williams. You've been unwell for at least a week, if not two. Following the phone call, Jessica informed Emily that she needed a Covid test asap and then demanded Emily get up. After some arguing and pleading, Emily eventually got up and within an hour they were both in the clinic carpark in a Covid testing queue. Emily slept in the car for the hour-long wait. Despite her tiredness, she roused easily for the test. The doctor took a swab of her throat and then put a swab in her nose, pushing it up as high as possible. Emily's eyes began to water from the pain. As soon as it was done, they went home to isolate until they received the result.

The next day Emily woke mid-morning, still feeling tired and she now had a dry cough. Just as she was about to get up to retrieve her phone, her mother entered her bedroom

'How are you feeling today?' Jessica asked, as she put the back of her hand on Emily's forehead.

'A bit headachy, that's all. No need to worry Mum. I'll get up and check my text messages to see if my Covid result is back.'

'I hope you don't mind, while you were asleep, I crept into your room and checked your phone this morning. So far no result, which means we still have to isolate.'

'Well Mum, as a matter of fact, I do mind. My phone is private. Please don't look at it again. I'll let you know when my result comes in. If it's negative, I'm going to the park for lunch. I feel cooped up. I need some fresh air.'

'Emily, you're going nowhere, irrespective of the result. We have to adapt to the changes in our lives and so far, you're not doing too well coping with the changes. By the way, how come you're suddenly interested in going to the park? Until lockdown, you've never shown much interest in going there.'

'I'm sick of isolation and the restrictions. I think it's

called cabin fever,' Emily replied as she pushed back her doona amid several dry coughs. Just as she was about to jump out of bed, her phone rang. She grabbed it when she saw her mother's arm reach for it. She looked at her phone then looked at her mother.

'It's the Department of Health and Human Services Mum,' Emily stated, handing her mother the phone.

'Mum can you take the call? I can't face this. I must have Covid. They wouldn't ring otherwise,' Emily tearfully requested.

'Em, they won't speak to me without your permission. Take the call and give them permission to speak to me.' After Emily had answered a couple of questions, she handed the phone to her mother. Jessica took the call and answered all the remaining questions. She was also advised to get a Covid test. Jessica turned to look at Emily's tear-stained face, 'the department told me they have to do contact tracing to see who you may have caught Covid from. I told them you haven't been in contact with anyone other than myself since lockdown, but before that, you'd been to the local shopping centre. Emily continued crying and coughing while Jessica went to get her daughter a glass of water. On her return, Jessica took Emily's temperature and sat down on the bed. 'Em, you have a mild fever and we're now confined to the house. We're in isolation so there's no more going to the park for lunch. You have to stay home for at least 14 days and then you need to test negative before you can go anywhere.'

'Mum, I need to tell you something. I met this gorgeous guy in the park and we didn't social distance. He told me he could get me a job. I got so excited I hugged him and have probably given him Covid. I feel so guilty and stupid. He mentioned social distancing and I said, stuff it, and chose to ignore it.'

'Emily, how could you be so reckless, hugging a stranger, of all people. You'll now need to contact him and let him know you have Covid.'

'He was such a cool guy, I don't know what got into me and worse still, I can't contact him because I don't have his details.'

'What! Emily, you are becoming reckless and your behaviour is really worrying me. Does he have your contact details?'

'Yes,' Emily replied as she buried her face in her pillow, her body convulsing as she sobbed.

'Oh my god,' Jessica said as she ran her hands through her hair.

'Em, turn around and stop crying. Let's work out what we need to do. The way I see it, I think you have two problems. I think you've had mild symptoms of Covid and we didn't notice them until now and you've become very moody. You've gone jogging to make yourself feel better. Would that be right?'

'Yes and I'm so sorry for what has happened. I feel so stupid. I have made such a mess of my life. Mum, what am I going to do about Lachie? He'll probably get Covid and I'm to blame. I can't tell him I'm COVID positive until he contacts me, *if* he contacts me.'

'My guess is, when he goes to the park and you're not there, you may not hear from him again. However, if he is legitimate about getting you a job and he does contact you, then you'll need to tell him about Covid and get his details to give to the health department,' Jessica advised.

'Now we need to take things one day at a time, so you can recover from corona virus, however long that may take. We've seen on the news how Covid-19 affects people in different ways and what the recovery can be like. Everyone is different. When you test negative, if you still feel miserable and weepy, I want you to see Dr Williams. I'm worried about your mental health. Will you agree to that?'

'I will. I'm so sorry for what I have put you through. I can't believe how stupid I am.'

'Em, I'm glad we can sort things out together. We now have to suck up fourteen days of isolation and then hopefully we both test negative. When you have fully recovered, we can discuss what you do next with your life. At the moment, your health takes priority both physical and mental and decisions shouldn't be made while you are sick. When you're feeling better, you might see things differently. We now have to wait and see how long it takes you to recover from Covid and how long the state of emergency will last. We'll deal with your studies later on. When one day blends into the next and we have no idea when Victoria will get out of stage 4, I think Netflix is looking like a pretty good option for the time being.'

The Unknown
Marlene Laurent
With thanks to the members of the
Caulfield Writers Group

Jane, Tim and Jacky sat around the dining room table planning their next holiday.

'Where would you like to go for a holiday overseas?' Mum asked.

Jacky and Tim began to argue.

'Now stop arguing and go to your bedrooms!'

Jacky and Tim ran to their bedrooms. An hour later, Mum popped her head in and asked, 'How are you going Jacky?'

'I'm hungry,' Jacky replied.

'Ok. Tim, we're going to have lunch soon,' Mum called out.

Over lunch they discussed plans for their first overseas holiday.

That night, at the dinner table, Jacky and Tim were feeling excited at the thought of sharing their holiday choices.

'Who wants to go first?' Dad asked.

'You can go first, Tim, as the youngest member of the

family,' Jacky offered.

'Why do you always remind me that I am younger than you, it's really annoying.'

'Ok Tim, stop arguing with your sister,' Dad interjected.

'Well, I was watching a show about endangered animals and it said that polar bears are critically endangered, as the ice is melting rapidly due to climate change and the presenter went on a tundra buggy in Canada and saw the polar bears in their natural habitat.'

There was a short silence as the family thought about Tim's suggestion.

'Brilliant,' piped up Dad. 'Mum and I thought it would be exciting to go skiing.'

'That's a great idea Tim, although I thought we could go to Borneo to see the orangutans, as they are also endangered but I guess I'm outnumbered,' Jacky commented.

They all went to the shopping centre to finalise their booking.

'I think the trip is in August,' Tim suggested confidently.

'Yes, there is a tundra buggy tour at that time,' Rob, the Flight Centre consultant, agreed.

So, the trip was booked for the end of August 2020.

~

'Are we going away for the Christmas break?' Tim asked Dad as they drove home from a cricket session. 'We could go to Mallacoota like we did last year. That was fun, and we could catch up with some of the friends we made.'

'Sounds good Mum and I were thinking of taking time off from work to be with you guys anyway. I'll check availability of the same place we stayed at.'

'Let's invite Grandma to come with us then she can be back in time for the Australian Open. We had a great day with her last year, and I really enjoyed seeing Kyrios play.'

'Why don't you jump on your bikes and go and ask what she plans to do.'

Jacky and Tim put on their bike helmets and rode around to their grandma's place.

'Hi you two, it's great to see you. I heard about your trip to Canada. That sounds amazing.'

'Yes, we're so excited.'

'Come in out of the heat and have a cool drink.'

'We would like to invite you to come with us to Mallacoota again,' Jacky added.

'I'd love to come. I have three tickets for two days at the Australian Open and was hoping you might like to come with me.'

'Grandma, that would be great!'

Jacky and Tim rode back to tell their mother the good news. Mallacoota was booked. As soon as school was over, the family packed their gear and drove there, even though Dad was concerned as a lightning strike had ignited a series of fires in East Gippsland on 21 November. Almost as soon as they arrived, they could smell the smoke from the fires. Despite that, they enjoyed catching up with their old friends.

'I've been listening to the latest updates about the bushfires on the ABC and it isn't sounding good,' Dad announced. 'An evacuation warning was issued for the East Gippsland town of Goongerah.'

'Do you think we should go home while we can?'

Mum asked.

'I think it's too late. Apparently, the Princes Highway has been closed and there's no way out.'

'Why didn't we get a warning? I knew the fires were in Gippsland, but thought we were safe,' Jane said with a worried look on her face.

'I guess we'll have to just stay put and wait to hear,' Dad said reassuringly. 'Let's get the kids to pack their bags in case we need to evacuate. I think they are outside playing with some of the other kids.'

'I'll get them,' Grandma offered.

'Thanks that would be good. Would you mind helping them to pack also, Mum?' Jane asked.

'Hey, Tim, can you find Jacky and come in for lunch, please?' Grandma called.

'Sure thing, Grandma, I'm hungry.'

While they were all eating lunch, Dad gave the latest update on the situation. Everybody began packing up. They all watched TV together in the evening and then went to bed.

'Mum, I can smell the smoke from the fires. How close do you think they are?' Tim asked feeling a little scared.

'The fires are not near us, so you don't have to be concerned,' Mum reassured him. 'Let's try and have a good night's sleep and see what happens tomorrow. Love you, night.'

'Night Mum, love you.'

Jacky and Tim talked for a while, as did Jane and Ted.

Everybody woke suddenly to the sound of the siren going off. It jolted them into action.

'It's really loud,' Tim complained, putting his hands

over his ears.

Dad stuck his head in the door, 'Quick, get up and get your food package and water from the fridge, that's a warning sound to evacuate. The fires are in Mallacoota. We'll do what we planned last night. Get in the car with all your belongings and we'll drive straight to the beach.'

Everybody threw their gear into the boot, jumped in the car and put on their seat belts. As they drove to the beach, the sky was black. There was smoke everywhere. The car lights came on.

'What time is it?' Jacky asked.

'Eight am,' Grandma replied. 'We'll be safe on the beach, no need to worry.' Although she didn't have a good feeling about what the rest of the day would be like.

'It's pitch-black. I thought it must still be night-time. It should have been daylight, but it's black like midnight,' Jacky commented.

Everybody in Mallacoota seemed to have the same idea. People were making their way in the direction of the beach. Some were standing on the pier with life vests on, ready to jump into the ocean.

'Can we leave our stuff in the car?' Tim asked.

'No, you'll need to take it with you,' Mum instructed.

'Why didn't they issue a warning on 29 December?' Grandma whispered.

'Well, we had planned to spend New Year's Eve on the beach, but not quite like this,' Dad said with a laugh.

'This looks like a good spot to settle,' Grandma suggested as people bustled to find a place to sit.

Someone came around giving out masks to those who didn't have them because it wasn't pleasant or healthy to be breathing in the black smoke that hung in the air.

As the day went on the sky, which was eerie black, turned to a deep red.

'Keep your masks on,' Mum said to Jacky and Tim. 'I know it's not fun wearing them, but I don't want you getting smoke in your lungs.'

Suddenly there was a deafening roar as the fire came closer and houses in the town caught alight.

'What's that sound?' Tim asked.

'Could be gas bottles exploding or just the ferocity of the fire, I'm not sure,' Dad suggested.

Everybody was scared but tried not to show it. Some people were crying, and others just sat staring into space, not knowing what was happening.

'The CFA will be working to protect us,' Dad said. 'Apparently the wind change drove the fire towards us in the middle of the night. The firefighters have moved to the beach, which is reassuring. They brought the masks that people have been handing out.'

Embers were falling down on the beach.

'Quick, get your beach towels out and use them to protect yourself from the embers. Let's wet them so that they won't catch on fire,' Grandma suggested.

That evening everybody celebrated as best they could and were kissing and hugging each other to see in 2020 and wondering what the New Year would bring. Some used their phone torches to add to the atmosphere, but not for long as they knew they may need them for emergency situations.

'This is scary but amazing,' Tim said.

That night people did their best to get some sleep after eating whatever food they had managed to bring with them. In the morning, the reality that they may be stuck on the beach for another day wasn't a pleasant one.

'Why don't you read your books,' Grandma suggested.

'It's all over the news, they can't leave us here too long, surely,' Mum complained.

With the smoke still blocking out the sun, a summer's day looked like night-time at the beachfront.

By the middle of the day, the sky remained reddish-orange and was thick with smoke.

'I don't have any more food to eat and I'm on my last bottle of water,' Tim said despairingly.

'Apparently Daniel Andrews said navy ships may be called upon to provide water and power to the area because the main road to the region has been closed off. Mallacoota can only be accessed by sea or from the air,' the guy next to them piped up. 'Although no serious injuries have been reported in Mallacoota, houses were going up in flames!'

Firefighters who had gathered at the shore, as the last line of defence, went around reassuring people all would be well, passing on the news that a change in wind direction had taken the worst of the fires away from the town and the beach.

'A lucky escape indeed, otherwise you would all have to get in the ocean,' one guy added.

Jane and Ted looked at each other. The relief on their faces reflected how worried they had been about their family's safety.

'How many people do you think are on the beach, Dad?' Tim asked. 'It's awfully crowded.'

'Some were saying there could even be four thousand,' Dad replied.

On Friday 3 January, army and naval personnel were deployed to rescue the stranded citizens. The HMAS Choules took some of the stranded holiday-makers off the beach and back to the Mornington Peninsula near Melbourne. The army arrived in Blackhawk and Chinook helicopters to help with the rescue. It was surreal to see the stranded holiday-makers walking with purpose despite their ordeal. They were so relieved that something was finally being done to rescue them. Their family was allowed to stay together and lucky to be chosen to be rescued in the first group, although Tim thought it would have been cool to be flown out by helicopter. The navy helped them onto the boat and directed them to where they needed to go.

'This will make a great show and tell holiday story,' Jacky said to Tim with a grin on her face.

'You can say that again,' Tim responded while tucking into a chocolate bar that had been given to him.

~

The holidays were over. Jacky and Tim were happy to be back at school as they missed their friends, although they enjoyed going to the Australian Open with Grandma. Term One began uneventfully on 28 January and was over soon as it was a short term of only nine weeks.

On the last day of term Tim and Jacky went to their rooms, threw their school bags on the floor when the heard Jane call out,

'Don't forget to bring your lunch boxes to the kitchen. We don't want a repeat of what happened last school holidays.

'That was a good science experiment!' Tim said with a giggle.

50

The school holidays were spent riding, playing on the trampoline or in the local park. Tim ran in to share the news before Jacky could.

'Mum, Grandma said we don't have to go to school next week. We can have a longer holiday.'

'Yes, that's right. I heard it on the radio, that's why we didn't go away this Easter even though we probably should have, to support some of the places that have suffered because of the bushfires. I think I'll just make a donation to help the koalas who survived. Apparently, it's best we keep a distance from others when we leave the house. It's called social distancing.'

'Can we go riding on the bike tracks?' Jacky asked.

'That's a good idea. Let's plan which tracks are close by and we could look up the weather forecast for good days to ride.'

That night Jacky and Tim told their Dad about their plans for the extended school holidays.

'You guys are great. My boss told me I have to work from home. That could be a challenge.

'Can we go to see the Star Wars movie showing at Pinewood?' Tim asked.

'Probably not, the theatres are closing, because they don't want large groups of people together.'

'That's stupid, after all we've been close with others at school,' Jacky whinged.

Later that night, after the kids were asleep, Jane and Ted discussed the threat of coronavirus.

'We need to keep the kids occupied, but we can't let them go to other houses. I don't think they can social distance at school and that's why the Premier is extending the school holidays. I don't ever remember that happening. How is your aunty going? I know she was having a test to see if the chemo has worked. What a time to be sick', said Ted.

'I'll give her a ring and find out how she is because we can't visit her, let's set up a Zoom session.'

When Jane zoomed her Aunty Sally and had a chat with her, the news wasn't good.

'She has to have another round of chemo to stop the cancer from spreading,' Jane confirmed.

The extended school holidays were quiet, and the family planned their exercise outings to keep fit and fill in the days. Everyone was enjoying spending time together.

'I guess we are all going to be fit if we keep this pace up,' Mum said as they rode along the Djerring Trail to meet up with their friends at the takeaway coffee shop.'

While the kids kicked a footy around on the oval, the adults chatted about the latest situation.

'We can't go out for lunch, and shopping has become a trial,' Jane's friend Sarah moaned.

'You can say that again. The stampede on toilet paper is ridiculous.'

'Yes, everything is on limited supply. Tasman Meats had no chicken, and I had to stand in the queue on crosses 1.5 metres apart. There were twenty shoppers in front of me,' Amanda chimed in.

'This is even crazier than being on the beach at Mallacoota escaping the bushfires,' Jane said. 'Let's hope it will be all over soon and we can get back to normal. I can't play netball, Tim can't play football, and Ted can't play golf. Even the AFL has been put on hold! Now that's serious,' she said as a joke. Everyone laughed.

It was the end of the extended first term school

holidays and the family were at the dinner table.

'What, we can't go back to school! Ye, ha,' Tim whooped.

'No, you can't, but you will be doing school work from home.'

'Really, how does that work?'

'Online learning – lucky you guys both have iPads. Dad will be working in the office, so we don't disturb him. He will have Zoom meetings with clients so you will need to keep the noise down.'

'How do they know if we are doing our schoolwork?' Tim asked.

'The teacher will be calling the roll in the morning. Dad will be checking on you and I will check your work when I return from work.'

'What do we do when it is recess and lunchtime?' Jacky asked.

'You can go out and ride your skateboards or bikes on the footpath and jump on your trampoline.

'Wow, that's awesome.' Tim said.

'Some of the learning is to be done independently, such as, projects,' Mum advised.

'You can choose your own topic to research.'

'I'm going to study the impact of the recent bushfires on the environment; I've read that it's a disaster. We're lucky we still have a home and food, unlike many of the animals and birds,' Jacky decided.

'There's a really interesting show on TV tonight about a dog that helps find the koalas that are left in the bushfire areas. He has been specially trained,' Mum said.

Jacky looked up the TV Guide. 'It's called *Bear- Koala Hero*.' They all sat down and watched the show together.

~

'Hey Mum, we're going to be allowed to go back to school soon because the number of Covid-19 cases has gone down,' Jacky said.

'That's because we have been doing the right thing, social distancing, staying home as much as possible and exercising on our own,' Dad added.

'Thank goodness,' Mum whispered to herself. 'That's great news.'

Even though we zoomed our friends every day, it's not quite the same as being able to play with them. I can't wait to see them,' Tim added.

'Elbows only, remember', Mum reminded them.

The last few weeks of the term seemed almost normal although the school now tested every child's temperature each morning and staggered the pick-up times. Jane continued to work at the aged care home. She was concerned for the elderly patients and about being at the coal face. Each night she had a shower on returning from work and debriefed with Ted when the kids were in bed.

~

'I'm so excited about our trip to Canada,' Jacky said as she was eating dinner.

'I was thinking we may not be able to go because of the coronavirus,' Jane replied, 'but it could still be possible if numbers fall soon.'

'That would be fantastic,' Tim joined in.

Ted just sat quietly keeping his thoughts to himself because he knew deep down that they wouldn't be going.

'Let's decide later on when it gets closer to the date.'

When Ted was on a business Zoom session one evening, Jane called Jacky and Tim to organise a surprise for Ted's birthday.

'It's Dad's 40th birthday soon, maybe we'll be lucky enough to have a party to celebrate. We might even be able to have a few friends over. The numbers have stabilised so they are going to lift the Stage 3 requirements. We are now allowed to have twenty people visit us. Let's go to the party shop and get some balloons and decorations,' Mum suggested.

'Can we call into the lolly shop on the way home?' Jacky asked.

'Good idea,' Mum agreed.

As they were driving home from their party shopping spree Mum had the radio on the ABC. Everybody sat in silence when they heard Dan Andrews announcing the restrictions had been changed. Only five people were now allowed to visit.

They all got out of the car in silence, disappointment written all over their faces.

'That's disappointing,' Mum finally said.

'Let's organise a special lunch.'

Despite not being able to celebrate with his friends and extended family, Dad had a fun day.

The number of people diagnosed with the coronavirus started increasing again.

'We're back to Stage 3 lockdown and online learning. I'm going to buy some material to make masks,' Mum said. 'Put in your order for colours and patterns.'

'Hey Mum I saw a great idea on Facebook for making masks out of socks. I'm going to give it a go with the new socks I have in my drawer from Christmas, but just in case it doesn't work, I'd like a floral pattern, please,' Jacky said.

I want polar bears but if you can't get that then my footy team colours will do,' said Tim laughing.

'Do we have to wear our masks when we are riding?' Tim asked.

'No just when we go out walking,' Mum answered.

That night at the dinner table Dad broke the bad news. 'The holiday to Canada has had to be cancelled.'

Jacky jumped up, ran into the bedroom and lay on her bed. Tim just said, 'We won't be able to see the polar bears or go on the tundra buggy.' That night no one finished eating their dinner.

'Let's have Uber eats tomorrow night,' Mum suggested, trying to cheer everybody up.

Do we get our deposit back'? Jane asked Ted when the kids were asleep.

'Not sure we'll have to wait and see.'

'Perhaps we could consider getting a dog to cheer the kids up and keep their minds off the gloomy future,' Ted suggested. 'I've been told you have to put your name on the list. Everybody's getting one.' He went off to put their name on the list.

When Jacky came out of her bedroom the next day her eyes were red and she had obviously been crying.

'I shouldn't be so upset but it is very disappointing. While I was in my room I started researching information for my project. This is what I found out:

'It's estimated 10,000 koalas perished in the bushfires, Jacky said wiping her eyes. 'I think the fires were just as bad as or worse than the coronavirus and giving up a holiday trip is not so important.'

'When you think about it, you are right,' Mum said. 'Let's see if we can donate some money to help the ones that have survived'

'I'm going to google my friends and get them to join me in a Skipathon to raise money for the survival of koalas,' Jacky said.

That night, Ted told Jane that his company was struggling and may have to put some workers onto JobKeeper. 'Maybe I could pick up some jobs mowing lawns,' Ted suggested. 'I think we should contact the bank about freezing the house loan. How is Sally going with her chemo?'

'She's sick most of the time. She's not going to have any more chemo after this. She may have to go into palliative care later on. I'm going to send her some flowers to cheer her up. I think we will be going to Stage 4 soon, whatever that means.'

They soon found out.

'We're confined to a five kilometre radius and we aren't allowed out between the hours of 8 pm until 5 am. People are being limited to one hour of exercise a day,' Dad reported.

'We still can't go back to school,' Tim groaned, as the holidays were extended by another week.

I thought it would be all over at the end of the six weeks.

Once the kids had gone to their room Ted whispered to Jane, 'I got an email from the Lost Dogs Home. They have a few dogs available if we would like to come and look.'

'That's great news Ted. It will cheer us all up. I guess we will have to buy doggie products online as all the retail shops are shut now,' Jane said thinking out loud.

'The kids are good at purchasing things online and it

will give them something to do.'

'Let's see if we can include Grandma. I know she is feeling very lonely not being allowed to visit us.'

That night Dad told Jacky and Tim about the possibility of getting a dog.

'The dogs that are available are on the webpage if you want to read about them before we go to look.'

'Come on Tim, let's go and see if we can pick the one we want. Let's tell Grandma to have a look and see which one she likes.'

That weekend Ted went to the Lost Dogs Home and found the dog they had chosen from the webpage. It was a black and white cocker spaniel.

'I don't know who is more excited, the kids or the dog,' Ted said to Grandma on the phone. 'You can walk it too if you like.'

'How are we going to choose a name? Tim asked.

'Let's all pick a name, write it down and put them in a hat. The one pulled out is the winner.'

Grandma won the competition with the name Lucy. So, Lucy it was. She very quickly became a member of the household. She was very active and kept everyone amused with her antics. It was fun looking forward to parcels arriving for Lucy.

'She's getting more mail than all of us put together,' Dad said, laughing. Just for fun they had the parcels addressed to *Lucy*!

The bad news came. Dad was put on JobKeeper. However, he was able to help Tim and Jacky with their projects and online school sessions.

'I think we should tell the children that Aunty Sally has gone into palliative care. They can't go in and visit but we could all talk to her on the phone and wave at the window. Maybe they could make a card or picture for her room. Fortunately, it's within in our five kilometre radius so we won't need to get special permission to visit her.

They all went to visit Aunty Sally. She was touched by the cards and messages the children had made and loved the fresh flowers. They took Lucy so she could meet her. They all chatted on the phone to her and sadly waved goodbye knowing this would be the last time they would see her. Jane was allowed to visit at the end but had to wear protective clothing. The funeral was online and even though it was held in the church five minutes away from where they lived, only Jane was included as one of the ten allowed to attend.

'Aunty Sally told me she wants us all to have a big party,' Jacky said with tears in her eyes, 'we'll cook her favourite muffins for the party, Mum.'

'Thanks, Jacky, that's so thoughtful.'

Tim just sat on the couch patting Lucy. 'I'm going to miss Aunty Sally. She was always such fun.'

~

'I'm so confused about the Stage 4 rules,' Jane said to her friends on their next Zoom session.

'Amanda, are you still allowed to have your nanny babysit while you and Bill work?'

'I think so, but we have to get our employers to sign a form to say we are essential workers. To be honest, I don't think anyone wants to give up their job if they've got one. Surely they are entitled to get a nanny in to look after the kids while they both work'

'Don't understand why the mower man can't come. I don't even know he's been half the time. I just leave the money in the electricity box for him,' Janice joined in.

'I hate wearing the mask when I go walking, especially as I have to wear it at work. It's no longer a pleasant experience but I understand why. Wow, border closures between states! Never thought it would come to that.'

Later that day Jane suggested Tim take Lucy for a walk. 'While you're gone, I'll go and do the shopping. Write down anything you want on the list before you go.'

'Why can't we go shopping with you, Mum? Tim asked.

'Only one person allowed to go shopping now, Tim', Jacky chimed in.

'That sucks,' Tim mumbled as he went out the door.'

~

The elderly at the aged-care home where Jane worked were getting sick and contracting the coronavirus. Even though families were expressing concern about not being able to visit their loved ones or being told how they were faring, the number of deaths was increasing. Jane continued to work in the home until the residents were evacuated. She was angry that people died because all the staff had been removed and the skeleton staff was left to their own devices. Jane was the only experienced nurse.

'Even when I told the doctor a couple of them needed oxygen and should be sent by ambulance to the hospital nothing happened. People should not have died.'

Ted told Jane she shouldn't blame herself. 'You did your best, now you need to focus on recovering yourself.'

Jane had contracted the coronavirus. She went into self-isolation. She felt exhausted most days and very lonely. Jacky and Tim had to go outside to get from their bedrooms to the kitchen and family room. They used to go to her bedroom window and blow a kiss to her. Eventually Jane was well again and given the all clear. She had to take sick leave while she was sick and then applied for JobSeeker. Jacky and Tim baked her favourite raspberry and chocolate slice to cheer her up.

'You are so brave Mum,' Jacky commented. 'I'm really angry with those idiots I saw on the news who refuse to wear their masks.'

As Jane sat drinking coffee and eating a piece of slice, she smiled, although she had tears in her eyes and said, 'I love you all so much. When I was sick, I realised I have everything in life to make me happy. It certainly is unprecedented times, but no matter what else happens, as long as we are together, that's all that matters.'

Five Poems
Sung-Ju Suya Lee

Swab

Crikey
Where's Dr. Seuss when it's the final curtain call
Put up your dukes, everyone's in this pandemic brawl
Leaps over sniffles, brace for the coronavirus squall
Can't escape, attacks the DNA scrawl
Hope, a mistake, what gall
Long list of unprecedented times, another wailing wall
Not waiting for plagues and flues to crank call
Assaults the mighty, the meagre, small, tall

Not a picky poison, wretchedness never lolls
Antiviral mutations, diseases and death never go AWOL
Drove early, across the urban sprawl
Sun hasn't broken the horizon, mate, follow the
            protocol
A long queue at the mall,
        from Melbourne
            to Mumbai
                to Montreal
Snaking in the parking lot, echoes of a screwball
Limp to the front of the line, more like crawl
A cough, whoa, money can't forestall
Want a cure, a jab, a stab, lysol, aerosol, alcohol
Distance, clean hands, a mask, survival or thrall
Stir crazy on menu, chewing up the wall
Time isn't on our side, researchers still trawl
Up your nose, a Q-tip as big as a cotton ball
Your nostrils widen, turns eyes into a waterfall

Can't win... Don't bother saying '... them all'
Try calling Buddha, Allah, Saint Paul
Ring the bell, no one's listening, especially city hall
Whole system, make that the world, needs an overhaul
Send out a recall, history don't care about our downfall
Dr. Seuss waves good-bye, behind the eight ball

Sold Out

Take a Ticket, The show is about to start
Right on time, Late comers will not be admitted
Never before seen, Not like the last time
Humans on display, 3-D glasses are best
Stage is set, Don't turn the channel
IMAX screenings for the blind, Surround sound for the
      deaf
Natural disasters on rotary, dial everything up to eleven
Weapons on sale, Scalpels are favoured
Bullets are shined, Arrows with bright feathers
Needles suck in blood, White powder flies over money
Liquids promise paradise, Family and friends promise
      lies
Addicts don't make habits, Choices crawl under the
      carpet
All knock you out, Oblivion is the prize

Pick your disease, Sucker punch the white cells
Go for your health check-up, Leave with dinosaur bones
Germs and genes mingle, T-cells drown in immunity
        hell
Pass the plasma down the line, Dust gathers souls
All seek a cure, No one highlights happiness
Spotlights on the heroes, Shadows for the dying
Standing room at the back, Behind pillars by the exit
        doors
Remote croaks, Batteries juice out
Projector breaks down, Film is blank
Your ticket is torn, Fine print is invisible
Everything is cancelled, Don't breathe
Forget unprecedented times, Our lives recycle
        nightmares
Homo Sapiens reduced to wholesale, Neanderthals have
        the last laugh
Life is 'sold' out, No refunds

Cure

Looking for a cure
Not a poem about happiness,
health,
wealth,
glowing cheeks, twinkling eyes.

Looking for a pill
Not for diseases,
moods,
longevity,
svelte, dimple free.

Looking for a mirror
Not for eradicating inequality,
racism,
sexism,
anti-Semitism,
potion for whitening, elixir for a billion followers.

Looking for great minds
Not for debating philosophy,
sociology,
political science,
fact over fiction,
talk shows, beauty contestants on world problems.

Looking for a saviour
Not for religion,
statues,
astrology,
law of attraction,
gofundme donations, any cause rallies.

Looking for nirvana
Not in unprecedented times,
death diseases,
slaughter executions,
meteorite extinctions,
free falling governments,
photoshopped selfies, instagrammed life.

Looking for a true me
Not inside my heart,
actions,
lifestyle,
romanticism,
tattoo sleeves, plastic surgery heaven.

Not looking anymore.

Ticker Tape

When did it start?
       Who put #1 up in lights?
Numbers race by,
       Increasing beyond believability
Too *much* to keep count,
       Breaks the brain in half
Not money,
       Not the stock market
Bulls take charge,
       Leave the bears behind
Can't cheat it,
       Can't escape it
Big Bang began,
       Infinity followed
Mother Nature was created,
       All live on Earth,
              With checks vs. balances

Chaos chased the world,
     Humankind advanced further
Humans record time,
     Humans delete common sense
Wins and defeats down in the history books,
     Names forgotten on tombstones
Cremations call for the latest human malady,
     COVID-19 stretches over Earth,
          Cemeteries overfill with souls
Catastrophe, calamity, cataclysm,
     Waiting for the next blow to the heart
Reuse the same excuse,
     Reprocess the next complaint
Time doesn't mind,
     Eternity expects the same story
DNA and our brains are the puzzles to bluster,
     Success slams lives attached on drip feed
Each day presents a gift,
     To live in an unprecedented time
Life started,
     Death ended it
Who's counting?
     Was it ever #0?
          No one remembers

Coffin with Your Coffee?

Welcome to the Sun & Shine Funeral Sanctuary
We're more than a monastery, missionary or mortuary
We treat you like a VIP, even in lockdown, guarantee
Excuse our vocabulary, we want to be legendary
No need to be literary, you can't go to the library
No need for a dictionary, just not ordinary
Here's the latest brochure, no fee, it's free
Browse online, it's not scary
Today, you're lucky, here's the honey
Half price, heck, we're so busy

We're not the military, but as a cautionary
Now it's customary, you know the corollary
A virus monster, third one this century
A devil's jubilee, before you know it, it'll be thirty-three
A deadly potpourri, a corona minestrone, a sinus
      spaghetti
Ha, ha, tiny? This one's the bee's knee
Nothing is arbitrary, it's mercenary
It's on a killing spree, add that to our history
Submit flu nominee, a stockpile in a centenary
Be wary, turns you into a zombie

What's the key? Make it a hobby
Here's latex gloves, sanitizers, mask, all sanitary
Tea or coffee? Place your order with the secretary
No tipping for him, not necessary
Have some candy, nothing dairy
No bats served here, but add as an inductee
First things first, that's primary
Here's the template for your obituary
Just write coronary, dysentery
You were macheted by the tooth fairy
You fought hard, like Rocky
That virus bully, life is temporary
No vaccine, SARS becomes your soul's amputee

No need to drive, we're next to the cemetery
Under the big Christmas tree, by the estuary
No snow, even if it's January
No problems, easy to bury
Flog the maraschino cherry, Hail Mary
Business is excellent, we are life's envy
Our services are truly visionary,
We franchise out to Sydney, Kentucky, Hawaii
Nobody but the best, the best of emissaries
Ricky Gervais will be your emcee
Eddie Murphy will do the commentary
Life of Brian will screen in the main marquee

Scroll down the tablet, a small plot of realty
One type of box, it's quite airy
We do rhinoplasty, no need for reality
Nothing in actuality, change your topography
Dress, not frumpy, smutty or corny, but funky or trippy
Go ahead, be greedy, go for Gucci
In death, dress in victory
Once you're dead, we burn the warranty
Six feet under, not solitary, but in good company
Reception culinary requirements, caters to all dietary
Casket of sherry, brie with mulberry

Only here for an enquiry, for an emissary?
A dignitary, retiree, or trustee?
It's easy, fill in form, don't need a seminary
Who is the payee? We accept any currency
First line, your name, and your ID
Whoopee, yippee or ducky!?
You don't say, Satyr, your name is me
Beastly, don't you agree?
You don't want to die, then home, flee
Out the window, goes carefree
Stay for another cup, showroom is for sightsee

The Good Boy
Andrew Marmont

I woke up feeling itchy and disorientated.

I opened my eyes and they slowly adjusted to the light. The sun streamed in through the curtains, and Adam was looking down at me with some concern.

'How are you, Charlie?'

He looked at my sores, which I could feel, sore and ugly, on the top of my head, and my nose. I stayed quiet.

'Not too good today, eh? I'll get Tess, see what she thinks.'

I blinked a couple of times more and felt sleepy. My head throbbed. I couldn't figure out why I had these sores starting to sprout on my head. They had grown worse and more numerous over these past few days. I could tell because they felt lumpy on my body.

Tess walked over with Adam following behind. She knelt down and touched my forehead gently. I grimaced. I knew she was trying to care for me; I often couldn't find my voice to show my appreciation.

'We might need to see the doctor again today. I'll call them when they open,' she said.

I hate going to see them.

It wasn't something I was used to. In fact, in the 18 months that I'd spent living with Adam and Tess, this was the first time I'd been to the doctor so regularly.

I still remember when Adam picked me up out of the foster home. We'd had formal introductions first and gotten along well. The home had dozens of others like me; unwanted, unappreciated, or simply, our carers couldn't look after us anymore. I'd been in this particular home for only a few days. Previously, I'd lived in another real home, like this one. I'd helped out on a farm, working with the animals and being out in nature. It was good work; tough, but enjoyable.

When they decided to move away, they decided they couldn't take me with them and dropped me off at the foster home.

A car ride later – it seemed to take ages, I slept right through it – I'd ended up there.

Adam and I met formally first. We'd had a chat – well, I remember doing most of the listening – and he said all the right things.

He and Tessa wanted to bring in a new family member to their home and wanted someone who was pretty relaxed. When the people there told me that I was moving to another home, I felt a sense of relief.

Adam came up to me, looked at me with his kind eyes, and brought me home.

It took me a while to be able to voice my opinion. But I felt like we had some good ground rules about all living together. They had become like my parents. I certainly felt that way, and now, the way they were caring for me, it was obvious they shared the same feelings.

All I wanted was to be a good son.

'C'mon mate, let's try having some brekkie,' Adam said.

I wasn't really hungry, so I didn't bother to answer. In fact, I just wanted to keep sleeping. I'd always enjoyed my morning meal. There wasn't ever a time when I didn't. But again, these were unprecedented times. I hadn't felt so poorly before.

I slowly rose up, stretched my arms, my legs, and moved into the kitchen. Breakfast always made me happy, and Adam was kind enough to prepare it for me. It was like our ritual; we always ate together.

It was a cool morning, but I tended to have my breakfast outside. I could clear my head and enjoy the breeze and the different smells of the flowers. Adam gave me my bowl of breakfast food. It looked like some tablets to take as well. I munched away as best I could, but managed only to stomach half my normal portion.

I looked in my reflection in the mirror and I could see some red marks across my nose and face. The sores had gotten worse overnight.

After finishing breakfast, we got in the car and headed to the doctors. I was reluctant. There was something about the place that never felt good. It smelt like sterile equipment. The doctor put her hands on my head, my arms and my legs. She then took a portion of my blood and came back a few minutes later.

'We've never seen this type of outbreak before,' the doctor said.

'I'm going to recommend a new medication. It's experimental, but it could really help Charlie.'

Tess composed herself, wiped her tears, and walked

with me back to the car. She looked at and touched my cheek again. I felt her cold hands; it felt soothing on my warm face.

We got home, and I took the new tablets. I didn't feel like doing much more for the rest of the day. Apart from some afternoon tea and a snack just before bed, I felt like going into a deep sleep, only rousing to drink some water and go to the bathroom.

It was exhausting. I continued to itch and scratch, but it just made the sores worse.

The next morning, I awoke to both Tess and Adam standing over my bed. I must have slept in; Adam always gets up before me, and I've usually had my breakfast long before Tess sees me in the kitchen.

'How are you, champ?' asks Adam.

Again, there wasn't much I could say that conveyed my pain, so I grunted softly.

My nose and face had bits of dry blood and crusty skin adorned my forehead. I felt hot around the head and neck. Perhaps a fever. I didn't want to move.

'Let's have some brekkie. C'mon bud!'

I wearily got up. My breakfast routine kept me going. Again, Adam had included a couple of additional tablets for me to take. They were bigger than the others. Could only eat half of my food, not really tasting anything.

I usually loved to walk around our local neighbourhood, spend time down at the park and be fairly social – you could say I was an outdoorsy type – but the sores had robbed me of my zest for these favourite activities.

~

Later that night, I saw Tess and Adam again looking

over at me, looking worried.

I saw them hug each other, Tess quietly sobbing, and Adam put his hand around her waist. They both gave me a little cuddle and a kiss.

'Sleep well, mate.'

I settled in for the night, only wanting the itching to stop.

The first thing I remember the next morning was hearing the distinctive shrill chirping of the birds outside. I hadn't heard that for the last few days. Something was different.

I blinked a couple of times. My body felt a little better. I no longer felt so lethargic. I didn't feel as itchy. It felt like a big improvement. I looked in a mirror and couldn't believe what I was seeing.

The sores had gone.

I jumped out of bed. It was time to tell my amazing parents about how much better I felt. I literally burst my way through the living room door and poked my nose into Tessa and Adam's room.

Adam was already out of bed and greeted me with open arms. He must have heard me scuttling across the house.

'Charlie! You feel better!' Tess jumped out of bed and gave me a hug. I let her touch my face and nose. The meds had worked. And now, after days of pain and itching, I felt like I was getting back to my normal self.

My body burst with happiness, my tail wagging with delight.

The Crooked Mile
Terry Morris

White corners of envelopes peep from the mouth of the letterbox, a sign of life inside the flats across the driveway.

Shadow by the window sees them.

'A message from our source on the Yarra,' he says.

Pinky doesn't look up from her tablet. If he sees that he's broken her train of thought, he'll nag her to fetch it. Like she's some kind of retriever. 'Just parkour over the balcony,' he'll say, 'sneak to the letterboxes,' – like there wasn't a whole wall of windows watching – 'and tumble back up to the third floor.' He laughs at gravity.

Pinky studies her question.

Shadow changes his spiel.

'We have to get it,' he says, 'before the snails eat it.' He thinks they all believe him that it's called snail mail because snails eat it.

The question on the screen is about why Isobel should want to be one of the crowd. The problem's in the words right there. Right now, everyone is in lockdown and crowds are illegal. Groups are illegal. Eighteenth birthday parties can't be had. No celebration, no getting drunk together, which would be awkward, anyway, with masks on. Especially the upchucking part.

No solitary drinking either, in a two-bedroom flat with the parents on hand. Even the formal is going to slip by with no occasion, no goodbye to school. Stuck at seventeen.

'It'll be good practice for the heist,' Shadow says.

So far, they've got code names, but they haven't decided what they'll heist. They have family meetings about it, which go roughly like this:

Gold, which is Mum because she didn't want to be Mr Blonde[1], wants something like a rare book, maybe a first edition of *The Lord of the Rings*.

Ruby says it should be for jewels or something, like the crown jewels.

Gold says this is a good idea because jewels are hidden in the coolest places, with locks to unpick, puzzles to solve, and lasers to evade. Best of all, the crown jewels are in a real tower. How cool is that!

She makes it sound like they'll actually meet Rapunzel.

Pinky thinks of the people who were abruptly locked in their towers. They could've grown their hair down to the ground so people could send food parcels up to them without having to go past the guards at the doors.

Shadow, which is Dad, because he chose Mr Black and then decided Shadow was cooler – why? only the Shadow knows[2] – says everyone has heard about the

---

[1]   *Reservoir Dogs*, film, directed by Quentin Tarantino, released 1993

[2]   'The Shadow', originally from *The Detective Story*

crown jewels and where they are, and they must be fake because otherwise they'd have been stolen centuries ago.

Sometimes work makes him grumpy. Sometimes that makes him go to the kitchen a lot for coffee, which leads to going to the bathroom a lot.

Ruby thinks having to guess where the jewels really are would make it all more exciting. They were probably in the Queen's bedroom. That's where she'd keep her jewels. In a pretty box with butterflies on it.

Gold thinks that people have broken into the Queen's bedroom a couple of times. Maybe the jewels are gone.

Shadow worries about attack corgis.

It wouldn't be a proper caper without attack corgis, Gold points out. Besides, Shadow could defeat them with his shadow. He'd call it up, 'Shadow, come forth',[3] and the dogs wouldn't be able to bite it.

Pinky thinks they should just hack themselves a win of humongous billions in the lottery and buy all the rare books and maps and jewels they want.

She refreshes her screen. The question is still there, still rubbish. If she uses the answer to explain about modern times, about crowds and masks, the markers might thank her for keeping them up to date, and give her extra marks. But probably not. There is always some trick to these questions. Besides, they probably still believe the

---

Hour, radio series, 1930,
https://en.wikipedia.org/wiki/The_Shadow
[3]   'Spy Shadow',
http://www.internationalhero.co.uk/s/spyshad.htm part of a forgotten cartoon show called *Super President*
https://en.wikipedia.org/wiki/Super_President

world is as they've always known it. Bushfires have never circled the whole nation. Melbourne has never lost its rain. Grandma Storm complains that the rain in Melbourne isn't what it used to be. There's almost no point carrying an umbrella at all anymore.

They are stuck like the captain on the *Titanic*[4] that one night when everything he knew was wrong.

If asked, Gold would start by saying that she preferred *Isobel On the Way to the Corner Shop*[5] to *I For Isobel*[6] because it was funnier.

On the way to the corner shop Isobel collapsed and got put in a hospital with all the other people with tuberculosis, and no one wore masks although they all knew tuberculosis was contagious, and heaps of poets and the occasional Studio Ghibli character had died of it back when it was called consumption.

Gold would talk all around the question without actually answering it. She'd be way off topic and lose heaps of marks.

If Shadow was asked, he would insist that she fetch the missive from the letterbox before he'd answer, and when she'd brought it, he'd just tell her to check the rubric and make sure all the boxes were ticked.

Like writing an essay was more a game of bingo than an offering of insight.

During the first lockdown, Shadow had explained his

---

[4]   *Titanic*, film, directed by James Cameron, released 1997

[5]   Isobel on the Way to the Corner Shop, by Amy Witting, Penguin, 1999

[6]   *I For Isobel*, by Amy Witting, Penguin, 1989

idea that exams were like heists. The object is not so much to learn as to beat the game.

'So, the goal is to beat the exam and never have to do it again,' Gold had added.

Right?

Now Gold frowns at her computer screen. She's lost her job and wants to learn a new skill during lockdown. Get employable. Maybe in advertising, which she might be good at if she put her mind to it, although she hates ads and the tutorials puzzle her. She's not very secretly hoping for a revolution to come and stop her from ever having to practice this stuff.

Gold's hair is dark, but when the sunlight gets on it, loose strands look darkest red.

'Come on,' Shadow says. 'It's a letter from Grandma.'

Pinky pops her earbuds in. She's stuck with the code name Mr Pink because Shadow thinks she's still the little girl who loves that colour, even though it was so long ago she doesn't remember it, and she certainly doesn't have anything pink in her wardrobe now.

She thinks of *Pinky and the Brain*[7]. This doesn't inspire a great sense of self-worth since she obviously isn't the Brain.

There's the rock star, though. Pink, the singer, who looks like she lifts weights when she's offstage, and totally owns the name.

Much better.

If gyms were open, she could lift weights, too, and start strong in the next crisis. If there wasn't a lockdown,

---

[7]   *Pinky and the Brain*, animated TV series, 1995, https://www.imdb.com/title/tt0112123/

she could get a job and have work experience when she went seriously job hunting. Of course, if there wasn't a lockdown, she'd be at school and just do her best at this because the path to uni and career was clear.

Instead, there is this obstacle, Isobel, who lived back when anyone could get a job anytime. Now there are nearly eight billion people in the world and rising, the jobs are being automated, and it doesn't take a genius to figure out where this is going.

The tune in her earbuds taps at her brain, a cheerful beat in a minor key, about going through the same ol' same ol' again until the dance becomes a trudge.

Her thoughts dance into a question translation. Isobel doesn't have to be in a crowd. She just wants to be able to blend into one, if there is one. She wants to be normal. Which is so last year. 'Normal' hadn't worked for everyone. It hadn't worked for Isobel. Poverty. Abuse. The prying. The questions. Greed had totally failed to be good.[8]

Something.

A spark.

A gleam on the beat, a shot slung out of the cycle.

Not the answer to the Isobel question, but the other one, the one about what to do when school is over. It's not the fallback, business studies, the fairly safe bet in the normal world, it's something about hospitals, but not in them. It's about something that should have been done, but wasn't, and is needed now.

It's to do with the finding of answers. She might have to switch to science.

---

[8]   *Wall Street*, film, directed by Oliver Stone, 1987

'Upstairs is taking a walk,' Shadow reports.

'Quick,' Gold says, and rises. 'Blow some bubbles for them to look at. Or wave.' She runs to the window and grabs the stuffed tiger to make it wave at the window. 'Pink,' she says, 'your mission is to run down with some of these little bubble bottles for them.'

'I can't go shoving weird little bottles at them,' Pinky points out. 'They'll freak out.'

'Oh.' The laugh goes out of Gold's face. 'It's so hard to know how to help people when you have to keep away from them.'

'Send letters,' says Shadow. 'Like Grandma Storm.'

Grandma doesn't care about *Reservoir Dogs*, which she says is too violent. She's always wanted to be Storm from the *X-men*[9] and this might be her last chance, and she's taking it.

'I'll get it,' says Ruby. Her code name is Mr Red, but they don't like to think of her as "Little Red" who gets swallowed by a wolf, so she's Ruby-Slippers[10], who will always find her way home. 'I'll go via the mines of Moria,[11]' she says, meaning the lifts. She grabs some

---

[9] *The X-Men*, animated TV series, 1992-1997 https://www.imdb.com/title/tt0103584/ Storm first appeared in the comics in Giant-Size X-Men, written by Len Wein, 1975 https://en.wikipedia.org/wiki/Storm_(Marvel_Comics)

[10] *The Wizard of Oz*, by Frank L Baum, first published by the George M. Hill Company, 1900

[11] *The Lord Of the Rings*, by JRR Tolkein, first published by Allen & Unwin, 1954

tissues to press the buttons with. 'And I'll water the pot plants while I'm there.' She takes the jug.

They watch out the window. The upstairs lady pushes a pram with the little one in it, and the walking one goes beside her in a thick coat against the cold. They turn and move slowly along the street and out of sight. A couple of magpies chase a crow away. Trees wave in the wind.

Ruby appears. She takes the letter out and studies the handwriting on the front, and then the back, and then stuffs it into a pocket where it'll be thoroughly crumpled by the time she gets back and they all read it, all crowded around a letter from Grandma.

Then Ruby waters the pots, looking carefully into each one to see how the flowers are growing. When the flowers grow, they hope butterflies will be attracted to them, but maybe they've already left it too late and the flowers won't bloom in time. It's nice, though, because they left a note near the pots to explain why they've been put there, and no one has knocked them down or tossed them aside. In fact, a couple of other, bigger pots, have appeared by the walls where it's sunny, and even a tray with wet sand for the butterflies to drink from. No one, not even a random person off the street, has wrecked any of it.

They feel very lucky about this.

Grave New World
Bala Mudaly

'Hey, don't shout, I can't hear you. Slow down, would ye.'

Ha, that's certainly Bianna. Who's she annoyed with now? Seems on the phone. I throw off the bedcover and get up in one determined motion. It's near ten by the wall clock. I feel a little unsteady, despite eleven hours of sleep. Been this way since a Covid-like flu hit me a week ago. Tested negative, as if that means anything. I make my way downstairs, gingerly holding onto to the rail. Barefoot. Bianna's whacking the pots in the sink.

'Hello dear,' I say sweetly and go over and peck her on the nape of her neck. She doesn't turn around. 'Who was on the phone just then?'

'My shitty son, of course. Who else?' She wipes her hands brusquely on her apron and glares as if I'm to blame. 'Ashbo skipped uni classes. Second time this week. He wants to be an authentic *black* man, he says. To prove it, he's in the thick of a BLM protest.'

'You mean there's a Black Lives Matter thing happening here in Bristol? Good lord, it's the ghost of

86

George Floyd's come to shake a fist at Colston.'

'I wish you'd be serious for once, Paul.'

Yes, I should temper my flippant habit, I think. I dish myself a helping of stewed apple cooked the evening before and plonk myself on a high stool at the kitchen counter. 'Shall I make you some toast, dear?' No response. Couldn't tell what Bianna feels about the protest.

'He phoned to ask me to join them. Not to miss history in the making', he said. 'Students mobilising the local folks and holiday visitors.'

'That should be some fun, love. Shall we?' I stick my bowl in the sink and start on the toast, making an extra slice for Bianna – just in case. I gaze out of the window. About time I tried some other way to get onto the good side of Ashbo, I think. He's so oppositional since I moved in with his mother, usurping their cosy closeness. He's been moody and sullen says Bianna, since she and her husband split. Out of loyalty to his dad, I guess. He insists on calling me a *whitey*. Hurtful, but I have to live with it as best as possible.

'Hey, watch the toast!'

I rush to turn on the extractor fan as the smell of burnt toast fills the air.

'Be more careful, dear, or you'll burn down the house one day.'

~

Bianna joins me over coffee and toast. We talk about the demonstration down at the Avon riverfront.

'You shouldn't be going out Paul, not just yet. The doctor said so. Look at you. Like the last man out of Auschwitz.'

'That's a hilarious image.' I laugh. 'Surely, I don't look like a Bristol scarecrow!'

She grins. 'But you do worry me, love. At seventy, you need to take better care of yourself.'

I find the slave history of Bristol unpleasant thinking about. Mostly skirt around it. But it's never too far from my awareness. Glaring landmarks all over the city to needle me. Like a nasty smell leeching from hidden drains. On school excursions to the docks and the maritime museum, we learned of Edward Colson, a wealthy maritime trader and owner of tall sailing ships who earned enormous riches for the citizens of Bristol. We stood at the foot of the man's statue in harsh sunlight and squinted at his large bronze face, his uncut locks falling onto his shoulders. Our great-grandfather's wealth, we were reminded, flowed generously through the veins of his descendants – me included. The truth did get to me in drips over time. Colston traded in slaves, buying and selling African men, women and children.

'I suppose with my Caribbean roots, the BLM movement should matter to me, Paul. But I really don't know if I can take the pushing and shoving by rowdy crowds,' says Bianna, buttering her toast. 'Makes me nervous. Wouldn't wish to catch this fearful virus.'

'You decide, love. I'm easy.' I go around and hug her.

'Ashbo's troublesome. He'll feel peeved if I don't turn up.'

I could tell she was feeling quite conflicted.

We're an odd couple. It's a fact. She's short, chocolate-brown, broad-nosed, frizzy hair and an earnest disposition. Me, pale-skinned, a Greek nose, lanky, shocking unruly hair, a set grin, and mostly irreverent. But her people and my people are bound by a grim historical reality. My ancestors traded her African ancestors to the slave colonies in the Caribbean as plantation labour.

'So, love, what you say?' I tog myself warmly and we walk to the ridge overlooking the Harbour Boulevard to get a sight of the protest. At least then Ashbo may tolerate me in the house. Who knows, he may still be sufficiently fired up at dinner tonight and speak about his experience of the day.

The summer light streamed into the kitchen, catching Bianna in a glow as she drained her coffee and handed me the cup. My turn to do the dishes. Reluctant or not, I usually got my way with Bianna. Today, I eventually won her over with one of my contrived jokes – *Why does Mr Monkey cross the road? Answer: His monkey business is on the other side!*

'That's absolutely stupid, Paul.' She laughed. 'You always embarrass me in company with such rubbish. But others seem to love it. Beats me every time. Okay, now go get changed. And leave the dressing gown you have on in the laundry. And about time.'

~

I stood momentarily on the back step, waiting for Bianna. The ungated dirt yard opening onto Raleigh Street just beyond was shaded by old pine trees. Two cars parked to the one side. When she finally emerged, Bianna *tick-boxed* me to ensure I was all set. Hat, mask, sanitiser, water, medication, binoculars, phone. She carried a small pack of cut fruit.

'No more than ninety minutes, right?' she instructed. 'Shouldn't miss your afternoon nap, dear. And remember *social distancing.'*

'Yes Sarge.' I saluted. 'Righto.'

Just down the street, we ran into energetic Evelyn, our neighbour from a few houses down, returning from walking her frisky spaniel. She had company. Her face lit up in surprise when told we were headed to the BLM protest.

'Oh, that sounds exciting. Can we go along? Sorry, this is Matt, by the way, my cousin, on a business trip from Melbourne.'

'Sure thing, why not,' I said, 'the more the merrier.'

She disappeared into her house to settle her dog while we chatted with Matt. He was a portly man in his fifties, with a ruddy face and an almost bald head.

'There's been some disruption to my flights, else I'd have been home a few days ago. Funny thing that I'm now to see a BLM protest here in Bristol when my wife told me only last night of similar big marches in Melbourne and elsewhere.'

I stepped aside to let a large woman pass by with a pram. We all spontaneously sneaked a peak. The baby was blissfully asleep. We smiled.

'That's right,' said Bianna adjusting her facemask, 'I caught a bit of it on the morning news. Protests about the ongoing detention of indigenous peoples, it said. Including kids as young as ten. Unbelievable. The police were rather active in discouraging the march taking place, apparently charging organisers.'

'Yeah, the government's not happy.' Matt frowned. 'They're in a bind with the pandemic not letting up.'

Just then Evelyn turned up, striding briskly. She had on a wide-brimmed floral hat, fresh lipstick and sunglasses. Bianna raised her eyebrows. We set off down the road that led generally in the direction of the waterfront, hoping to catch the protest march somewhere in the vicinity. It was a question of trusting our noses to get us there.

~

As we turned into Burtle Road, we were rather surprised to see many people ahead, perhaps with the same intention as us. I noticed Matt's interest in the buildings here, old and care-worn, but still bravely standing up to some modest restoration and use, low-rental shops mostly.

'Remind me later, Matt, to tell you about the graffiti all along here, especially about the illusive artist, Banksy.'

Intrigued, Matt nodded. Burtle Road was cobbled and relatively narrow, and the pavement even narrower. Unbroken lines of parked vehicles at either kerb compelled us to take to the middle of the road. Fortunately, not much traffic troubled us which I thought was unusual. The women set the pace. Bianna was never happy going on a walk with me as I seldom kept up, which frustrated her no end.

'You have to get your heart pumping,' she always insisted.

~

When we got to the steepest point in the road overlooking the docks, I suggested we stop for coffee at the High Point Café, which had seating on the second-level balcony. My suggestion was quite brilliant, I thought, since we'd have an expansive view. In fact, from across the road, we spotted a clutch of patrons on the balcony, standing and gesticulating towards the waterfront. Faint rallying cries drifted our way.

'No dear,' protested Bianna, 'we don't have time for coffee.'

'But why? I thought this was as far as we intended to come to catch a glimpse of the demonstration. The balcony is the best vantage point.'

Matt looked a little uncomfortable and embarrassed.

'I'm sure, love, Matt and Evelyn would like a closer look at the crowd.'

Evelyn murmured in full agreement.

It's annoying how Bianna tended to change her mind. I felt my jaw tighten. And what's more, my facemask wasn't helping matters.

'Okay then, if you say so. But let's stay close. And if we're separated, let's meet at this café.'

There was visible relief on all three faces. So, we kept going, now with more purpose and haste. But some misgivings remained with me. What if we get sucked into a chaotic throng? What of the pandemic and the safe distance rule?

~

The voices grew ever louder. We turned a corner and found ourselves in College Green, and there ahead of us was a milling crowd of protesters, mostly animated college students by my assessment. They held up placards of all sizes and wordings: *Black Lives Matter*; *White Silence is violence*; *Stop killing us*; *Fuck face masks – I can't breathe*; *Fight modern day slavery*; *Remember the Uighurs*. I couldn't quite make sense of the one that said *Shut this crap down*.

Evelyn scanned the restive crowd. 'We certainly look like a bunch of fuddy-duddies,' she concluded with a look of amusement.

Bianna chortled, adjusting her facemask yet again.

92

'No hope of finding my son in this melee.'

We fell silent for a moment, wondering 'what next?' I felt uncertain to venture any closer. While many protesters wore masks, even from where I stood, I could tell several didn't. But then, neither Matt nor Evelyn came protected.

~

Obviously responding to some signal, the protesters began moving down Colston Avenue, shouting slogans and responding in unison to the rallying call: *No justice … No peace. No justice … No peace.*

'Okay, I'll stick around here. You all feel free to join the protest. Go on, then.' Bianna frowned, clearly undecided. In the end we mostly stuck together, trailing at a slow pace. Matt had his phone out busy capturing the rare moment for family back in Australia.

The police in orange vests and masks stood by in large numbers but didn't discourage the march in any visible way. The media, too, were well represented. Microphones on extended arms were thrust into the faces of protesters, seeking their comment. For me the situation was one of chaotic movement and cacophony – quite giddying. To compound matters, the summer sun was at its zenith and the air was still. A weariness crept upon me. I drained my water bottle and plodded on, transferring my backpack to my other shoulder.

~

Bianna was in her element. She certainly got into the spirit of the protest, shouting repeatedly from the rear *'Black Lives Matter'* in her shrill voice, thrusting her fist into the air. I felt a little embarrassed myself and feared she may want me to emulate her. Not exactly sure if the colour of my skin inhibited me. Or my age. It never struck me before that Bristol was home to such a lot of black people. How many were direct descendants of slaves, I wondered, and how many foreign students.

We had not gone for more than twenty minutes when the throng began slowing down. 'What's up?' asked Matt.

'Don't ask me. Perhaps a pitstop,' I joked, reaching out for Bianna's water bottle.

'Goodness me,' shouted Evelyn, who was tall enough to look over the heads of those in front. 'We've stopped at the Colston statue.'

Exactly right, I thought. Makes sense. The protesters intend to make some sort of dramatic anti-racist statement as a finale. We stood far back gaping as they rapidly formed a cordon around the 17th century statue of Edward Colston.

'Tell me about this guy, Paul', whispered Matt. I told him the little I'd been taught at school, the koshered version which painted Colston as a wealthy shipowner, merchant and trader in slaves and commodities who made Bristol prosperous. Certainly not the infamous stuff
94

Ashbo often spat into my face.

'You're no different from the rest of the imperial white pigs,' he would rage. 'How can you not know? Fuckin check it out, if you're doubting me.'

He would storm out, dismissing pleas from his mother. Of course, he just hates my guts. Clearly, he's talking rubbish. Eight thousand black people branded, herded onto Colston's ships like live animals. Certainly not that many? Fake news, alright? It didn't take me long, however, to verify the truth of the narrative. I felt ashamed.

I so wished now that I could mend my strained relationship with Ashbo. Poor Bianna finds herself to be the meat in the sandwich.

A forest of mobile phones shot up into the air to capture the moment. The protesters egged a daring few to attack the life-size statue mounted on a ten-feet high pedestal. Two men with aerosol cans were given a leg-up. Bronze was soon sprayed red to the accompanying chants of *murderer, murderer, die!* More hands joined in. Ropes were thrown to them as they balanced precariously on the ledge of the pedestal. The statue was firmly secured, and several rope ends were flung to folks waiting to grab hold of them. Young men and women began to tug and pull the ends. It alarmed me just speculating on the outcome.

Throngs of spectators in the high-rise office blocks across Colston Avenue leaned out of open windows and balconies. Many shouted encouragements, but a vociferous few hurled abuse. *Vandals! Vandals! You black bastards! Why trash history?*

'Hey, where you're going?' I shouted in alarm as Bianna broke rank.

'Ashbo, Ashbo,' she screamed, pushing her way towards the statue which was already rocking on the pedestal and giving way.

'See, that's him.' Evelyn pointed, almost jumping out of her shoes. 'Bianna's son, the tall black guy on the ledge up there with the afro beard and hair. Yellow top.'

'Jesus, Bianna, come back, Colston's about to fall. Someone stop her, hold her back.' I shouted to no one in particular as I thrust myself forward, pushing bodies aside, reaching out in a frantic effort. But my little Bianna simply disappeared into the roused and surging crowd. My chest heaved, I felt faint with panic and lost focus.

'I think he's spotted his mum,' said Evelyn reassuringly, taking hold of me and handing me her water bottle. I noticed Ashbo scramble off his perch shouting at someone below.

To my great relief, Bianna re-emerged through the crowd propelled by the determined arms of Ashbo.

'Now stick with Paul, you hear,' he urged in a grim voice. 'The fun's over, see, so go back home. All of you.'

I said, 'Hi Ashbo, thanks.' He simply looked away, his bearded face dripping with sweat, eyes large and wild. Blotches of red smeared his yellow top. He swung around and disappeared back into the action.

Bianna sighed, looking woebegone. 'I just wanted my son to know I came. But now he seems annoyed I came.'

I hugged her and commiserated. 'But that's not it, dear. He was simply scared you were about to be smashed by Mr Colston landing on his head.' Evelyn and Matt smiled and made sympathetic sounds.

Just then there were loud alerts from the guys on the pedestal. *Get back … Get back … Keep clear, give way. Going,*

going ... Fearful cheering and clapping rose into the air. A brazen Indian myna took off from a bush nearby, clutching a greasy McDonald's wrapper. Right there, to our great consternation, Colston, bound and lassoed by ropes, gave up his lofty standing with reluctance, swaying and tilting precariously at first, then leaning into a decided fall.

Whohoooooo went the voices in unison, as people stood on their toes to capture the remarkable descent into ignominy of one of Bristol's long touted benefactor.

The tuggers dropped their ropes and scattered as the bronze monolith hit the ground with a metallic thud. For a moment we four stood in stunned silence while the protesters cheered and danced in great glee, stomping on the statue. One puny girl even knelt on Colston's neck as her photo was taken.

~

'*How the mighty are fallen,*' I whispered, with a mock solemn face. Bianna gave me a puzzled look and grinned.

The police stood by expressionless.

'No social distancing happening here,' shouted Matt almost into my ear.

I suggested we retreat to the safety of the pavement across Colston Avenue. 'Should we start walking back? I expect the protesters will soon drift away.' Not only was I starving, but I was beginning to worry that a storm was brewing. A sudden breeze caught a line of plane trees along the avenue in disturbed motion. After a sultry morning, the sky was rapidly turning ominous. Hmm, I thought, the white man's god may have been angered.

'A few more minutes,' pleaded Matt. 'I want a close video of Colston on the ground.'

We left the women chatting and edged closer to the statute resting on its back. A bunch of protesters nearby appeared to be consulting. I was certain to see a 17th century man of fame and fortune in a pose of supreme arrogance or triumph. What a shock then to discover that the sculptor had turned Colston into a heroic, contemplative person - forehead all creased, a face deep in thought and cupped in hand. An image of someone leaning heavily on his staff – almost mimicking Rodin's sculptor of the *Thinker*. For some reason, I felt really angry. What deception! You callous and miserably bugger. Lie there in the dirt, for all I care. No sympathy from me.

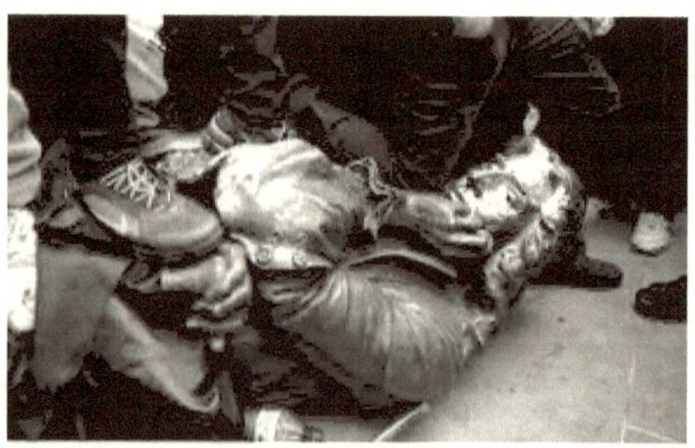

'Hey Paul, look – the women are being interviewed.'

I look up and noticed that both the cameraman and woman interviewer had *Bristol TV* across the back of their vests. Matt and I rushed across just as Bianna was speaking. I laced my arm in hers for support. She said her son had been in the thick of the protest and that she had Caribbean roots.

'And what about you?' The woman thrust her microphone at Matt, 'As a white Britisher, are you for this BLM protest?'

'I'm Australian actually, here visiting. My wife was in a similar rally in Melbourne only the other night.'

That seemed to grab the interest of the interviewer.

'Was it also about George Floyd and black Americans?'

Bianna couldn't resist cutting in. 'Haven't you heard of black deaths in custody? And indigenous kids as young as ten in detention?' She frowned.

A little ruffled, the interviewer turned to Evelyn.

'How come few facemask and little social distancing? Isn't it irresponsible for this rally to happen in the middle of a pandemic?'

Evelyn, caught unawares, appeared startled and almost tongue-tied.

'If not now, when?' shouted a scruffy heavyset black student, elbowing in and simultaneously thrusting his placard into the camera, almost knocking the cameraman off his feet. The next second, he'd vanished. I couldn't stop laughing until our attention was drawn by fresh commotion from where Colston lay defaced and grounded. The TV crew rushed to the spot.

They were moving the statue, rolling it along the

ground in the direction of the wharf. Many spectators near us gasped obviously guessing the intention of the protesters.

~

Bristol Harbour was only a few hundred metres from where we stood. We rushed across the road into an open grassed public area, found high ground, and watched the bronze hulk being dragged and rolled with the combined effort of many enthusiastic hands. Again, I noticed police standing witness, one of them with a large camera documenting the event.

For a brief moment, Colston was teased and dangled at the water's edge and then unceremoniously dumped. We heard a mighty splash as the sculpture hit the water. Those leaning over the wharf taking photos, jumped back with a scream, and a spontaneous hurrah rose to heaven.

We set off home in a reflective mood. Matt and I tried keeping up with the women. We spoke little. Guilt and potential consequences of shrugging off Covid-19 surfaced, but I kept my mouth shut.

The evening news on Bristol TV, as expected, carried full coverage of the protest and the dramatic toppling of the Colston statue. I gasped when I saw a shot of the statue-less pedestal. It reminded me of the shock I had on seeing my face for the first time after removing my long-cherished moustache. I felt completely nude. My facial landscape had changed.

Bianna and I waited with anticipation to catch ourselves on TV. It didn't happen. But what caught our attention was an irate local member of parliament questioning why the police had stood by and did nothing. Heads may roll, he added.

Hackles up, Bianna fumed. 'We can't let that happen, can we, Paul?'

'Hang on, love, there's the Chief Constable come on. Let's hear his defence.'

'You'd agree it was a volatile situation,' he said 'People were angry. Intervening or arresting anyone may have provoked a major confrontation. But let's be clear, we don't condone vandalisation of public property. Not in the least.'

Ashbo wasn't home for dinner. Bianna fretted. He surfaced for breakfast two days later. Although greatly relieved, Bianna couldn't help but be terse with him, wanting an explanation. He seemed preoccupied, but he sat with us and nibbled at a piece of toast. He even made passing eye contact with me.

'Mum, got to tell you both something.' Ashbo sounded grave. I'd bet he's in some kind of shit. Watch it, Paul., I cautioned myself, not the time for wisecracks.

'A few of us have had calls from the police advising us not to leave Bristol for the next few days. I guess the bastards used racial profiling and contact tracing to get us.'

Bianna, dropped her knife and looked at me with fear in her eyes. 'Could be nothing serious, routine police check,' I said to reassure them. 'But if the situation needs legal advice, we'll help you there, Ashbo.' The tension somewhat eased, we chatted about the protest and how it had gone. I wondered aloud if the protesters had further plan.

'Hell yes, I just remembered,' Ashbo perked up. 'Will you both come with me into the city centre tomorrow morning? I don't promise, but there may be a surprise awaiting us.'

How could we turn down such an intriguing invitation, especially when I'm included?

~

So it was that we stood at Colston's vacated pedestal for the second time in a few days, in the midst of a

confounded but largely amused crowd. I couldn't believe
my eyes, for there on the pedestal someone had installed
a statue of a magnificent black woman in a defiant pose –
fist high in the air. 'Just look at that.' I beamed, hugging
Bianna.

All she could do was utter 'Oh my god, Ashbo. Oh,
my god, how superb.'

Ashbo laughed with pride. If he personally had a hand
in installing this visual statement, he did not let on. 'That's
the statue of my college friend Jen Reid, one of the
protest leaders,' he confided. 'Cast overnight in resin by
one smart artist.'

The media was out in full force, and the police were consulting on their phones, clearly flummoxed for the moment. I doubted if the statue would find favour with the city fathers. It did, however, make me wonder if memorials ought to be installed to stand for all time when life and all else in the universe were so transient. Should traditionalists be allowed to cling to a white-washed history of colonisation and revere a dark and callous man like Edward Colston?

'Angel above, that's unbelievable.'

'What you on about now, mum?'

'It looks like Angela Davis. Almost a splitting image of her, I tell you.'

'Huh?

'No, you'd not know her, son. Much before your time.'

But *I* remembered the Black Power movement. Those heady days in the 1960s and 70s. It all came rushing back, names of firebrands like Bobby Serle, Eldridge Cleaver, Stokely Carmichael and Angela Davis.

On yeah?

'Yeah, you check her out, Ashbo. People say history repeats itself. So do pandemics. Old folks like us are certainly familiar with *unprecedented times.*'

I was tempted to add my bit to impress him. Something lofty and wise. *Ha yes, the tide of history is punctuated with high moments of black and brown struggle against white domination. There's been many a Geronimo, Jandamarra, Gandhi, Spartacus, Mandela, and Martin Luther King who'd risen and fallen for human rights.* Brilliant sentiment, I thought, but maybe just a little over the top for now. But worth remembering for a later chat with Ashbo. I felt pleased, but my smile went unnoticed beneath a scruffy homemade mask.

Extinguish
Robert New

'DA-AD!' Johnny heard his son, Matty, scream at the top of his lungs. 'CASSIE PUNCHED ME.'

How the hell was he meant to get any work done with the two of them needling each other all the time? It didn't seem fair that his wife got to go to work each day. Though, God bless her, Annie was a nurse and as selfless as they came. He shouldn't be upset that she was getting out. Still, Johnny had to admit he was jealous; not only of her getting out of the house, but also the time away from the kids. Matty and Cassie were twins, but somehow the 'twin-bond' had steadily worn away since their birth seven years ago.

'DA-AD!' Matty screamed again. *Ugh.* Johnny clambered upstairs to the children's living room.

'WHAT?' Johnny shouted as he reached the top of the stairs. He felt himself breathing harder from the exertion. Damn cigarettes. They were his crutch, and during this infernal lockdown it was near impossible to get to smoke them. *Never in front of the kids.* That was Johnny's one ironclad rule, but the lockdown meant the
106

kids were with him twenty-four seven. There was no escape. It was an intolerable situation.

'Cassie hit me in the arm,' Matty cried, glaring at his sister.

Cassie, for her part, looked guilty, but in her usual defiant manner defended her action. 'He called me a poopyhead.'

'I've had enough of this,' Johnny said icily. His kids knew that tone, and they wilted. They seemed to find it scarier than him shouting. 'Matty. Stop. Just stop. This is too much, okay? Okay?'

'Yes, Dad,' they replied in unison.

'Matty. Go downstairs and play on the Switch. Cassie. Stay here. I'll put on a movie for you. What do you want?'

'The icy movie.'

Johnny sighed, it was always one of those two. 'Which one?' he asked.

'The second one, with the forest.'

'Fine.' Johnny set up the movie to play from a Blu-ray disc. He was grateful it wouldn't wear out like the tapes he'd watched repeatedly as a child. Life seemed simpler then. God, he needed a cigarette.

Johnny's mind flitted back to the first time he'd smoked. He was sixteen and at a party for his best friend, Imran. There was a girl there, Nishka, whom Johnny had a crush on. He'd followed her round to the back of the house. When she lit up and offered one to Johnny, he couldn't say no. He'd coughed a bit, but the smile Nishka gave in response made up for the discomfort. She made it clear she'd recently broken up with her boyfriend. Johnny's heart had leapt at the news. She was letting him know she was available. He'd asked her out just before the call for speeches. They'd dated for seven months. She taught him which milk bars and service stations were lax about checking ID's. Even now, he could still remember her grin when Johnny bought his first pack and they'd split it. They'd made out for what seemed like an age that afternoon. It was ample reward.

'Right. Matty, Cassie's all set up. Wait, why are you still up here? *Go downstairs.*' Johnny's icy tone returned.

Matty withered and skulked downstairs. He was such a sensitive kid. All it took was a telling off for him to seem like his world was collapsing. One time, he'd grazed his knee after coming off his bike. It had taken minutes for the first speck of blood to appear, but Matty had seemed convinced he was bleeding to death, or at least had a major injury. Thankfully, the magic of a bandaid had miraculously made the wound feel 'all better'.

That wasn't even the worst response though. Anytime Johnny and Annie yelled at each other, Matty was convinced they were about to divorce. Cassie, on the other hand, barely reacted. If the anger wasn't directed at her, she was fine. Heck, she was amused if it was directed at Matty. Surely there must be some happy middle-ground response?

Johnny walked downstairs with his son. 'Matty?'
'Yeah, Dad?'
'You're not in trouble anymore. I just need to separate the two of you for the moment. I've *got* to get back to work.' Johnny's big project was due in two days and he was a week behind. The thought just made him want a smoke. Nicotine always seemed to fuel his productivity.

Annie had tried to get him to quit. But her efforts were to no avail. She'd first tried talking constantly about her patients in the ICU. It was surprising how many were there due to smoking related illnesses. Which, Annie reminded Johnny, weren't just cancer and emphysema, but also heart disease, stroke, diabetes and even arthritis. The argument had failed. Johnny knew the risks, surely everyone did, but Johnny had never suffered from any of those illnesses, so the argument didn't seem relevant. Next, she'd tried focussing on the financial savings quitting would bring. Johnny was a two-pack a week smoker and the seventy dollars they'd save each week could pay for a family holiday each Christmas. That, at least, had some appeal. Getting away for Christmas day would be great. It would spare the multitude of homes they had to visit to make sure all the grandparents, and aunts, and uncles had a chance to give the kids a present. By the end of the day the kids were exhausted and their adrenaline high from presents and candy canes would inevitably lead to an almighty crash. Johnny couldn't remember a Christmas which hadn't ended with the kids in tears and Johnny gasping for a smoke. Last Christmas he'd promised Annie he would quit. But deep down he knew he hadn't meant it. He'd lasted a week that time. It wasn't even close to the three weeks he'd lasted when the kids were born.

Johnny made himself a coffee. Caffeine wasn't as good a stimulant as nicotine, but at least it might help his brain fire up. The sound of the automatic machine grinding the coffee and brewing the rich espresso Johnny favoured was a joy. Johnny liked watching the first drops fall into the small, pre-warmed China mug he used for his coffees. It seemed like just from the sound, he could tell exactly how much time was left from the pushing of the start button, to the coffee puck being swept from the group head. He knew every moment of the cycle.

Aah, that first sip. It was almost as good as—

'Dad,' Matty said quietly, just loud enough to interrupt Johnny's thoughts.

Johnny took his coffee over and sat on the couch next to his son. 'What's up, my little man.' With his son's sensitivity, it was best to try lightening the mood.

'I'm sorry. I know I shouldn't have called her a poopyhead.'

Why did kids always remind you of exactly which bad word they'd said?

'I know. It's over now. How's your game going?'

Matty's face brightened up. 'So good. I've got nearly enough diamonds to buy the shield. That will allow me to fight the aquamonster and gain a new heart piece.'

Johnny nodded, knowing he'd never understand the appeal of such a game. It was so open, so non-linear, and the more you achieved, the more bosses you had to fight. What was the point? Why wasn't there only one boss to fight? That was more true to life. Like his boss, Carl. That guy seemed itching for a battle.

Carl had warned him his performance on this project was being monitored. He'd hated him for that. All he did now was second-guess every decision he made. Surely, the average of his work should be considered? Why were the highs barely acknowledged and the lows emphasised so much? The bulk of what he did was good, solid work. That's what he should be judged on. Not set up for failure like this, with an impossible timeline.

Johnny took the last swig of his coffee and returned to his study. He regretted not keeping the coffee for when he was at his desk. Two monitors of data and an open document he was writing didn't fill him with hope he'd be able to get the task done. When his leg started shaking, he was sure, if he could only have a cigarette, and the kids remain quiet, he could make decent progress over the next couple of hours.

Remain quiet. That was interesting. The kids *were* quiet. Each was likely to remain doing their thing for at least ninety minutes, until Cassie's movie ended. Maybe, just maybe, he could sneak outside? He'd never done that when Annie wasn't home to be a guard. But just this once?

Johnny went to the bookcase and pulled a large dictionary off the top shelf. He took his pack of cigarettes from behind it and replaced the book. Good. The lighter was still in the pack with the cigarettes. He headed outside.

The cold air meant nothing when there was the promise of a smoke. Johnny went round the side of the house, away from the living room windows where he might be seen. He walked past the kitchen to where there was a windowless wall provided by the side of the garage.

The first drag was always the best. Something about lighting the cigarette, watching the tobacco and paper catch alight and those first sensuous curls of smoke appear. It was beautiful. And then there was the satisfaction of the inhale. The extra warmth and texture of the smoky air felt as good as taking the mask off after his daily walk around the block.

Johnny took another drag on his cigarette. God that felt wonderful. It was why he'd found quitting so hard. He took a few steps and snuck a peek through the kitchen window. Cassie hadn't come downstairs. Matty was still playing his adventure game on the big screen TV. Good. They'd been utter ratbags today. He deserved the break from them.

Johnny ducked further round the side of the house, away from the window, and took another long drag. He blew smoke rings as he exhaled. *Bliss.*

He recalled Annie making him try patches. They hadn't worked. He'd lasted two weeks that time, but he knew from day one it wouldn't last. His addiction wasn't just to the nicotine. It was the act. That's what Annie couldn't understand. It was the ritual.

Matty suddenly appeared next to him. 'What are you doing, Dad?'

Johnny felt like a guilty schoolboy. He hadn't been so ashamed since he was a teenager and his older brother had dakked him in front of his friends.

Matty looked at him with such alarm and then a deep, lingering sadness. Johnny was shaken to his core. The poor boy.

'I know w-what that is. That can kill you,' Matty said, his voice quivering. 'I-I don't want you to die. I-I love you, Dad. I'm sorry I … I won't do it again.'

Johnny's heart broke as he realised his son was crying – mourning the loss of his father as though it was about to happen, as though it was his fault. Such a sensitive soul, Johnny reminded himself.

'It's my last one. I swear it.' For the first time Johnny felt like he meant the words. All those times he'd tried to quit, he'd failed because of his focus on the act. The switch flicked by his son meant he'd now focus on the consequence: that gut-wrenchingly sad expression on

Matty's face. Johnny couldn't bear being the cause of that. He'd never smoke again.

The Light
R. Andrew Russell

'Seven days and nights the sky was bathed in ever-changing convulsions of colour, demonstrating God's fury.' The minister raised both hands high in the air as though calling for this sign to reappear. 'Unprecedented times indeed. Everything made of metal attracted lightning bolts and stunned anyone unwise enough to touch them. People fell from the sky or were crushed and maimed by evil machines suddenly gone berserk.'

Children seated in the front row of the chapel followed each graphic detail with wide-eyed attention.

'Every ungodly idol man had created was destroyed. There was drought, famine, pestilence and lawlessness. These events were the consequences of man's greed and disregard for the ways of the natural world. Only those who embraced nature by tending to the land and working with organic materials were allowed to survive.'

Sage suppressed a yawn. The minister's sermons rarely strayed far from this theme. Some of the congregation believed her father's work trod a fine line between the excesses of the past and current ways of piety. Others, like the minister, were firmly of the opinion he was an ungodly person who should be whipped out of town.

~

The soil was dry, compacted and had the familiar musty smell of decay. This layer of soil was less than two metres deep. As her father had explained, it was too shallow for any delicate electronics to have survived God's fury, but there might still be other useful things. He used the minister's words 'God's fury' but maintained The Light was the result of an instability in the sun and not associated with divine intervention. Sage was employing her favourite tool, a spoon, so worn through constant use the handle was most of what remained. With painstaking care she scraped away the next layer of plastic and cloth fragments and was rewarded by the smallest glint of shiny metal or perhaps glass. She breathed deeply, forcing herself to work slowly and methodically. It was so easy to destroy a valuable new find in the rush to satisfy one's curiosity She thought back over her prized discoveries, the set of small screwdrivers, the solar-powered calculator, the windup alarm clock.

With trembling hands, she cleared around the edges, trying not to damage it. Eventually, the object was free and could be washed in a bucket of water. This was a wonderful discovery, a complete pair of glasses! They were hardly corroded, even after their long burial in the rubbish tip. Cradling her valuable find in both hands, Sage hurried back to the dilapidated barn where she and her father stored and repaired the things they uncovered.

'Father, look at this,' Sage exclaimed as she bounded through the doorway. Excitement immediately turned to concern when she saw her father. He had been unwell for the past two days. Now he looked much worse, deathly pale and sweating profusely. It seemed as though he'd been dismantling an old radio. The soldering iron was still heating on the charcoal burner. However, all his tools had been pushed to one side as he hunched over the bench, wheezing and gasping for breath. After a fit of body-convulsing coughs, Sage caught sight of bright red blood staining her father's handkerchief.

'Did you see Dr Sawatsky like Mother told you to?' Sage asked accusingly.

'Sure I went … a lot of good it did.' Samuel shook his head dismissively. 'He just said there's a lot of this kind of thing going around.' Following a few moments of thought he added, 'Gave me some herbs. I'm supposed to boil them up and inhale the steam.' After witnessing another spasm of coughing and gasping for breath, Sage gently pulled her father to his feet and guided him the short distance to their home.

Sage's mother was overcome by the sight of her husband, and her worry showed as they both put him to bed.

'I've never seen your father this bad. If only there was something else we could do.' Sage realised she must act quickly. Only a week earlier their neighbour, Frank Little, had come down with something similar. He barely lasted four days and was buried on Saturday. She straightened up.

'I'll go and see the doctor myself. I've a new battery for him anyway.'

~

Dr Sawatsky was delighted to see Sage when he discovered what she was carrying. The homemade battery was the size of a large loaf of bread and wouldn't fit inside

116

the ear torch, so it had to be connected by long wires. After satisfying himself that it worked, Dr Sawatsky turned to offer Sage a half sack of flour, the previously agreed price for a new battery. Sage held up her hand to stop him.

'You know Father's desperately sick?' Dr Sawatsky let out a long breath as he sat down and then nodded slightly in agreement.

'I've seen a few similar cases recently. I must warn you, his outlook isn't very hopeful.'

'Surly there's something you can do for him?' In the silence that followed, Sage handed the doctor the pair of glasses she found that morning. Dr Sawatsky carefully folded and unfolded the arms, nodding in approval as they moved smoothly. Then he took off his own glasses and swapped them for the new pair. First with one eye closed followed by the other, he looked at his outstretched index finger. Sage guessed that he was gauging the power of the lenses. With a sigh, he laid the glasses aside and addressed Sage.

'You excavate things that have been buried in the ground for many years. More than anyone else in the village you must know that the time before The Light was an age of wonders.' Pointing at the ear torch he went on, 'In that age they could make things like this and batteries small enough to fit inside.' When Sage was young, her father had told her all about The Light, more to explain the thinking of the authorities than anything else. The village elders didn't want people to know what life was like before The Light. They didn't want people to hanker after things that were lost. They thought it was the extravagant and dissolute lifestyle of those times that brought down the events of The Light as punishment.

Lowering his voice in a conspiratorial manner, Dr Sawatsky continued. 'When I was apprenticed to the herbalist, old Dr Morrison, he passed on to me some special medication dating from before The Light. There's hardly any left now. Of course, it's irreplaceable and so it can only be used in the most exceptional situations.' The doctor gestured for Sage to remain seated as he crossed the room to a cellar door and, with obvious reluctance, climbed down out of sight. When he returned he was carrying two small cardboard boxes. They were water damaged and faded, but still in good condition for something that must have dated back to before The Light. 'These are called antibiotics. They can kill the germs which cause illnesses. When they were first manufactured the dose was one taken three times a day, with plenty of water. Over time, even though they've been kept cool in my cellar, their effectiveness has reduced. I recommend your father takes double the dose until they're all used up. Keep them hidden and tell no one, you understand?' Sage nodded, thanking the doctor profusely and promising a year's supply of batteries in exchange for the medication.

As she hurried home deep in thought about her father, she was stopped by the Graber twins, Isaac and Abram. At school they had enjoyed throwing their weight around. Now they were part-time bailiffs at the Court House. Their new position gave them even more scope for bullying.

'Hey Sage, there's been a complaint about you talking to the kids after school. They say you have been putting all sorts of forbidden ideas into their heads. Ideas about what you think things were like before The Light.' With this, the twins grabbed an arm each and dragged her towards the Court House. 'We've been told to lock you up overnight so you can appear before a gathering of the Assembly in the morning.'

'My father's sick. I have to attend to him.'

'Not our problem. Explain the situation at the Assembly tomorrow.'

~

Two metal cages were built into the Court House to accommodate people accused of minor crimes such as poaching and petty theft. Now, apparently, this stretched to spreading seditious gossip. Other than Sage, the building was empty. Two flickering oil lamps cast long shadows across the wall opposite and there, hanging from a nail, was the key to the cage. She assumed many people before her had reached through the bars to gauge the distance. It was tantalising, but the key was well out of reach.

It hadn't taken the illness long to kill Frank Little. Sage knew she must get the medication to her father without delay. Fortunately, she hadn't been searched. Looking around, she tried to think of some way to escape.

Using a sewing pin she always carried stuck into the bib of her overalls, she started to unpick the wool from the hem of her pullover. When she judged the length of wool would reach across the corridor, Sage turned her attention to one of the magnetic clasps her mother had used to secure the shoulder straps of her overalls. The clasps were another rare item excavated from the tip. Her pin came in useful to remove the stitching holding the magnet. After tying the magnet to the end of the wool, she tossed it across the corridor. Eventually, after many tries, she was able to snare the key with the magnet and pull it from the nail, across the floor and into her outstretched hand.

In the almost total darkness, she managed to return home without being seen.

'Sage, where on earth have you been? What with your father's illness I can do without worrying about you.'

'I visited Dr Sawatsky and he gave me this special medication. He insists we don't show it to anyone else. Father must swallow two of these white discs three times every day, with plenty of water.'

Sage demonstrated how to pop a disc out of the plastic foils.

'After you've given Father his first dose of medication, hide it carefully. Then, could you please help me by repairing my pullover and overalls. I must get back to the Court House. I've been locked up there for spreading forbidden ideas.'

Deftly, her mother reattached the magnetic clasp and made a quick repair to the hem of the pullover, now a little shorter. With a despairing look, she hugged her daughter before going back to her husband's bedside. Taking some food, Sage returned to the Court House cell. After locking the cell door, she threw the key and hoped it would look as though it had simply fallen from the nail.

~

The Court House was full for the meeting of the Assembly. For most people in the village, there was special interest in the day's proceedings because they benefited from bottles, tins, clothing and other items Sage and her father unearthed. They had a stake in a continued supply of treasures coming from the tip.

Councillor Reynold, who also served as Minister of the Chapel, convened the Assembly. He read from a sheet of handmade paper.

'Sage Mortimer, you are accused of subversion by spreading contraband items and ideas from before The Light. We all know God intended The Light to eradicate these kinds of abominations and with them the profligate squandering of the earth's riches.'

Reading further down the page, the Councillor itemised some of the incarnations of evil. 'You have described all manner of flying vehicles, vehicles which travelled over ground, machines which contained the contents of whole libraries, devices to record and reproduce images and voices of people distant in time and distantly separated. These activities set people hankering for the times before The Light and bring discontent to the community.'

He paused as though waiting to see if Sage would deny any of the accusations.

'In the past we have tolerated the activities of you and your family but now they must stop. The purpose of this meeting is to decide if all of you should be banished from the village.'

Adopting a defiant stance, Sage addressed the Councillor.

'Councillor Reynold, you run the village grocery business, don't you?'

'Everyone here knows that to be the case. How is this relevant?'

'Your store sells eggs?'

The Councillor waved a dismissive hand.

'If you don't have anything sensible to say, you should sit down.'

'If an egg is worth 23 cents, how much would seven

eggs cost?'

'Young woman, I'm not a school child to be quizzed with such trivial questions.'

'But running a business you would need to be able to do this kind of calculation. So, what's the answer?'

When there was no reply to the question, Sage pointed an accusing finger.

'I've heard you use a machine for this, one that was made before The Light.

There was an awkward silence and then quickly, as though hoping most people at the meeting wouldn't work out what was going on, he answered, 'On reflection, we may need to reconsider the gravity of your crime. Because God's love is infinite, perhaps a final warning would be appropriate.'

Campaign for the 40-Hour Week
Gordon Smith

This is a story of the campaign for the 40-hour week, a campaign waged by the unions with unprecedented swiftness and tenacity after the end of WW2 – a tale of the events of the time

The year 1946 saw the beginnings of a new war, the Cold War, which was really no more than a weapons race between Russia and the USA. The Communist Party in Australia was making its presence felt, much to the chagrin of the leader of the opposition Liberal Party, Bob Menzies, who was trying to have the party banned. The Australian Railway Union (ARU) led by the communist secretary, JJ Brown, together with other communist-led industrial unions, began the push for a shorter working week, from 44 hours to 40 hours, together with other claims.

I was an apprentice fitter and turner at the Newport railway workshops and was working in the turnery on a milling machine, when a series of union mass meetings began taking place during lunch times. JJ Brown addressed a couple of these lunchtime mass meetings on a platform erected for the purpose outside the carriage shop.

At first, I did not take much notice, but one lunchtime, instead of reading a book, I went and had a look. The union shop steward for the ARU at the workshops was a big bloke by the name of Mr Treasure, who always opened meetings with a short address before he called on JJ Brown to speak. JJ Brown was the secretary of the union. He was an imposing, stocky, red-faced man, and always opened his address with the word 'comrades,' which even allowing for its Russian overtones, I felt it to be an appropriate form of address under the circumstances.

He then went on to speak loudly to the audience of about one hundred employees. Not all of those present were members of the ARU, some were tradesmen of various unions of workers employed at the workshops, the Amalgamated Engineering Union (AEU) to which most fitters and turners belonged, as well as other unions, electrical, boilermaker, coppersmiths, carpenters, upholstery and foundry workers to name a few. I had in fact been asked to join the AEU early that year but declined, mainly because as an apprentice I was not required to join. Belonging to a union was not compulsory at the Newport Workshops, but my understanding was that the majority of workers in those years saw fit to be a unionist.

After attending one of the first of these meetings, where voting was always by a show of hands, I learnt two valuable lessons. The first of these was when I picked up a newspaper on the way home on the day of the first mass

124

meeting I attended and read the report in the newspaper of the meeting. I found it to be grossly distorted and bore little resemblance to the conduct of the meeting. From that day on, I have always been very wary of the truth of reports I read in newspapers.

The other lesson I learnt concerned the apathetic attitude of some of my workmates. After attending a number of these mass meetings, and returning to my workplace, I was usually asked: 'What happened at the meeting today?' In reply I would give them a short account of the decisions taken at the meeting, which usually engendered a disgruntled response.

I continued going to these 'combined union shop meetings' as they were called, which meant that the vote of those workers who belonged to unions other than the ARU was legitimate. One day, when I returned to work after a meeting, I was asked the same question: 'What happened at the meeting today?' This time, however, I finally got fed up and replied: 'Why weren't you at the meeting?' They said that they did not like communists, to which I said to them, in no uncertain terms for a third-year apprentice: 'Well go and vote against them!' Whether they did or not I was not sure, but they never asked me again. I must admit that of all the motions that were put to the meetings, I don't remember one hand going up to vote against any of the motions.

I think that despite the communist presence, most workers were in favour of the 40-hour week and other benefits the communist unions were seeking, although not all unions were communist-led.

Mr Menzies was Prime Minister of Australia for a short period from 1939 to 1941, but was overthrown and eventually became the Liberal leader of the Coalition and Ben Chifley, a former locomotive driver, became the Labor Prime Minister in 1945. Menzies hated the Communist Party and did everything he could to negate their policies and ban the party.

One day, the news came through that Mr Menzies wanted to speak to the workers at the Newport Workshops at noon. He was, however, not allowed to address the men inside the workshops, so Menzies had to do so outside the main gates in Champion Road. I wandered out there at lunchtime, where a sort of rostrum had been set up for him to stand on. There was quite a good gathering of men waiting, but he was late and when he eventually arrived, he stood up on the rostrum and apologised, saying he had been held up at the Bendigo Workshops. Immediately someone yelled out: 'I don't know why you bothered to come at all!'

Menzies, a well-built man with greying hair, was known to be a exceptional orator and quick on the repartee. Quick as a flash he answered: 'Well, why did *you* come, was it to hear something that might raise your intelligence level, which might be an impossibility for the likes of you?' With that he began his speech in his upper-class accent, to which the men listened in complete silence, not willing to risk another interjection and another equally stinging reply.

He spoke about working conditions and a little about the Communists, but he was treading a fine line, because in criticising the Communists he had to be careful not to alienate the workers many of whom, although not communists themselves, had sympathy for the party and its fight for better working conditions for all workers. The

126

whistle sounded, and we all returned to work from what I thought was an interesting opportunity to meet and listen to what Menzies had to say, although even at that stage in my life, I was not one of his admirers.

Eventually, on 7 October 1946, in support of claims relating to annual leave, the basic wage, overtime rates and the 40-hour week, there was a one-day strike, so a day when I could not get to work. After a couple more mass meetings, with JJ Brown really going to great heights of strident oratory, with his face getting redder and redder all the time, the result was that the meeting voted for more strike action. JJ Brown was the skipping champion of Victoria for quite some time, so despite the red, blood-filled face, he was a very fit man.

Two weeks later a strike was called and all railway employees, not only the ARU, but the AEU and all the other unions, tramway employees as well, went on strike and all services were suspended for nine days. My father managed to get a lift in a friend's car every day of the strike to his work at Cox Brothers in the city. Most people who worked in the city and other workplaces were able to get to work by car or bicycle. Apart from going on a bike ride every now and again, I filled in the rest of the nine days playing with my model trains and doing odd jobs around the house. It appeared that after the strike, engineering unions in some industries continued with the strike, but I was unaware of this, and members of other unions went on strike in sympathy with them.

Quite often during the lunch hour, JJ Brown was back again conducting strident mass meetings with demands for the 40-hour week, better pay and other improved conditions. On 14 April 1947, employees were withdrawn from the railway's power station at Newport, which resulted in the loss of power for the whole suburban train system and all suburban trains ceased to run. This, of course, meant that once again I could not get to work, and I mucked around at home for a few days.

Knowing that there was a small engineering shop called Georgian Engineer in Heidelberg not far from home, I got on my bike and went and saw the manager. I told him that I was a fourth-year apprentice fitter and turner with VR and could not get to work; could he give me a job? He said yes, I could work for him while the railways were on strike, so I started there the following day.

Georgian Engineering was run by two great blokes, George and Ian, which was where the name came from. I worked on a small lathe, screw cutting a 14' long, square thread, table adjustment screws for small wood worker's tables. That was no trouble as I had already screw cut in the turnery last year.

I enjoyed working there for the whole time of the strike that at last ended on 8 May, a total of twenty-five days. There was a little talk about whether I might like to remain with them and finish my apprenticeship there, but I said no thanks, and after thanking them for taking me on, they said that they had been happy with the time I spent with them. So, it was back to Newport and work as usual, but there was no indication from the government that the unions' claims would be agreed to.

On the morning of 9 September 1947, *The Sun News-Pictorial* had the following headline emblazoned across its front page: **UNION SATISFACTION AT 40-HOUR WEEK**

In a text box below the headline were the following words: Trade union leaders generally expressed satisfaction yesterday with the 40-hour week decision, announced by the Arbitration Court to operate from the first pay period in January1948. Employers' organizations said they accepted the Court's decision and would loyally abide by it, but they emphasized that increased costs would have to be borne by the public. There was a lot more on the front page about the decision, but those words were the most pertinent.

The railway union and other workers here at Newport and elsewhere, led by JJ Brown, had won the long fight and all the mass meetings had served their purpose. In my apprenticeship so far, I had learnt about the many facets of a working life in the railways and more. Most importantly, the truth of the slogan 'in unity there's strength', demonstrated to me by winning the war and winning the 40-hour week. I had learnt not to trust what is written in newspapers and of the apathy of some workers when moves are made by unions, to better their working conditions, communist or not. All of this was a part of learning about life that provided for me a good background for the path my life would take me in the future.

One day I received a memo from the Apprentice Master, Mr Curtis. informing me that because I had been unable to get to work at Newport from my home in Rosanna when the strikes shut down the railways on many occasions; I would have to make up the time lost to complete my apprenticeship. A one-day strike and a nine-day strike in 1946, twenty-four days in 1947, making a total of thirty-five days. The memo informed me that I would have to work as an apprentice for an extra thirty-five days into 1949, before I completed my five-year apprenticeship and received my tradesman's fitter and turner certificate.

This was a huge disappointment, quite apart from delaying the day I could call myself a fitter and turner without the word *apprentice* prefix; it also meant that I would have to wait to get a full tradesman's wage of about £6 odd. However, I really knew I was a tradesman fitter and turner when I received my first pay packet sometime after Wednesday 16 January 1949, which contained my first, tradesman's weekly award wage of around £7 and, at the same time, my tradesman's certificate. So ended a wonderful five years of learning a trade, which was to provide me with a very exciting and wonderful life.

Very soon after I became a tradesman, I joined the AEU, the metal trades union that all fitters and turners in VR belonged to. The 40-hour week, and the other improvements to working conditions that were won in this campaign have their affect even on present day working conditions.

This story is a shortened extract from my book *Learning a Trade 1944 to 1949.*

Into the Dust
Erica Tippett

0 kilometres

From where she was standing, she couldn't see the start line. She could only just see the track. The sun beat down overhead, it must be close to the start time. She shook her hands, arms, then legs, trying to alleviate the tight feeling in her stomach. The starter gun fired. Its echo reverberated through the trees. She saw the puff of smoke rise and dissipate. The group of men on the course pressed forward. The shuffle quickly became a jog, then a run. They were off. Stamata was left standing there, wishing she could run with them.

0 kilometres

The next morning, Stamata stood at the start line. Alone. 'Take your mark,' she called out. 'Get set. Go!' Stamata imagined the starter gun and leaped forward. She started at a jog, then increased her speed to a run, keeping pace with her imaginary counterparts. She could picture the men in their race attire – long sleeved cotton tops and pants with running shoes made of canvas and leather. They were a far cry from the shoes she had found and mended. She dodged rocks on the road, along with bicycles and the odd horse and carriage. Whenever she was passed by a vehicle, she averted her eyes from the staring male onlookers. She imagined herself somewhere in the middle of the field, falling just behind another runner, keeping pace in their slip stream. She was familiar with the road from Marathónas to Athens, but she didn't know it well.

~

10 kilometres

Stamata's pace slowed as she neared the first hill. She wiped dust and sweat from her forehead with the back of her hand. She scrunched up her nose as the sickly-sweet smell of sweat filled her nostrils. As she climbed the first rise, she passed a goat tethered to a young boy. He was pulling at the rope, trying to get the goat to follow him, but the goat stood strong, munching the leaves of a bush. Stamata mumbled to herself, 'I am strong, like that goat'. A smile turned her lips from the straight line that had held tight since the start line. She looked up to see the top of the hill. In her mind's eye she saw runners scattered over it like flowers in the spring meadows she remembered from when she was a child.

~

Stamata stumbled out of the factory, embarrassed and forlorn. Her head hung low as she walked towards the next employment prospect in this godforsaken town. But it was no use, there was no work in the packing shed either. She returned to her meagre hut to the sound of the baby crying. Her son was playing in the dirt on the floor. 'What's wrong with you?' she scolded. 'Can't you hear your brother's cries?'

The boy shrugged; his bony shoulders poked out from beneath his ragged clothes. 'He's always crying,

Mama. If I pick him up, he cries. Same if I put him down. I wanted to play.' He rearranged the stones on the floor.

Stamata picked up the baby and rocked him gently. She sat down on the bed and fed him her milk. He ate hungrily.

'What's for tea, Mama?' the boy asked sweetly.

Stamata looked blankly ahead. Tears rolled down her cheeks. Try as she did, she couldn't answer.

~

11 kilometres

By the time Stamata reached the top of the hill she was panting hard. She felt the sting in her side of a stitch and breathed out more forcefully so she could breathe in more deeply. Her legs felt heavy. She focused on putting one foot in front of the other, repeating to herself, 'left foot, right foot', over and over again. She let the momentum of the downhill propel her legs faster and faster, but didn't let them get out of control. She knew that downhill was dangerous for injuries. The breeze through her hair felt glorious and she relished the feeling, closing her eyes for a moment.

~

'Looking for work?' The stranger asked.

Stamata adjusted the scarf on her head, peering at the man. 'Yes,' she said.

'There are good jobs in Athens. Government jobs. Once you get them, you're set for life, they pay very well,' the stranger said.

'How can I get to Athens, when I have no money and no job to pay any in the first place?' Stamata sighed.

'I've seen you run around here, haven't I?'

Stamata blushed. 'Well I ...'

'You know there's a race next week starting in

Marathónas. You should enter.'

'But I'm a woman!' Stamata cried. 'They don't let women run.'

'That's silly,' he said. 'If you were a man, would you try?'

'Of course. If I was a man, I'd win. But I'd already have a job and wouldn't need to.'

'But you might do it anyway,' the man smiled. 'Here, take this coin. Run the race. Change your destiny.'

The stranger placed a drachma in Stamata's hand, bowed and left. She watched the man disappear into the crowded street. She turned the coin over in her hand. It felt heavy and cold.

18 kilometres

Stamata gained speed through the woods. The shade overhead gave her energy and she felt like she was running on air. She settled into the rhythm. The canopy overhead thickened. Stamata didn't see the tree root pushing up from underground until it was too late. Her shoe caught the edge and she felt her ankle turn. Pain stabbed at her and she stumbled, then fell, skidding to a stop, stones tearing flesh from her knees and hands. Her heart beat wildly in her chest. She imagined bystanders sniggering at her and calling out 'that's why women aren't allowed to run,' and 'serves you right, you should go back home'.

Stamata tried to stand. She looked around for something to steady herself, but tree trunks bent and swayed, and the road blurred in her vision. She clenched her eyes shut, grimacing at the shooting pain. 'Don't panic, Stamata,' she whispered, 'you just twisted your ankle a little on a root in the road. You have overcome so much more pain than this. You will finish this run.' She took a deep breath in, counting to seven, then let it out to the same number. Her heartbeat calmed. She blinked her eyes open slowly and brought her left leg in close to examine the damage. There wasn't any visible damage to her ankle. She studied her knees. There were stones, a little blood and grazes. But they were shallow. She reached for a fallen twig and pulled two leaves off, gently brushing at the stones. She studied her palms.

~

The boy screamed. Stamata ran outside with the newborn baby, asleep in the sling she'd tied to her chest only minutes before. The bike lay on the path, front wheel still spinning.

'Mama, I'm hurt, I'm hurt,' he cried.

'It's okay, my child,' she said bending to him and unfurling his fingers. His hands were bloodied. She turned them over and saw skin torn from knuckles. 'Come, come inside and I'll make it better.' She smiled at her son. Tears ran down his face and dropped silently in the dirt.

18.2 kilometres

Stamata grimaced as she pushed herself upright. She hobbled over to a tree and snapped a small branch. She used it as a walking stick. As she walked slowly forward, she gained more movement and confidence in her ankle. She threw the stick aside and began to jog again. Her jog quickened to a run as she went down a gentle slope. There was a little pain, but she could bear it. 'You are strong. You can do anything.' She repeated these words as she picked up the pace and forgot about the pain.

The trees thinned and Stamata came up on a view across the ocean. There were tiny puffs of cloud punctuating the hazy blue sky. She took in a deep breath and smelled the salt and seaweed. After a few more kilometres the road turned inland once more. She knew she was reaching the halfway point of the marathon. She slowed on approach to a crossroad. There were no signs and she went ahead to the right as it seemed like a continuation of the road she was on. After a little while the scenery started to change. Stamata slowed her pace and looked around. She came to a stop near a low fence. 'What should I do?' She leant against the fence and felt her breathing slow and return to normal.

'You can't stand around here all day,' she scolded. Stamata was alone. The only sounds she could hear came from her. Heart pounding in her ears; breath going in and out through her nose. The heat from the sun beating down was stifling. Stamata raised her hand to shade her face. She noticed movement beyond the fence. A blur of colour. 'Hello?' she called out. 'Can you help? I've lost my way.' Stamata felt her heartbeat quicken. Her mouth was dry, and she was struck by a sudden thirst. There was movement again. A flash of green near a tumbled down shack, beyond the old olive grove. Stamata climbed through the fence. 'Please? I'm running to Athens. I've come all the way from Marathónas,' she blurted out. Then shook her head in dismay. 'I could be the first woman to run the marathon,' she said with a sigh, then smiled. A shaft of sun penetrated the darkened ruins, and Stamata saw two eyes under a messy head of black-brown hair. 'It's okay,' she said. 'I won't hurt you. Maybe you can help. You look like you know this place well. Do you know which is the main road back there? I turned up this road, but it doesn't feel right.' The boy moved slowly out of the shadows. Stamata gasped.

He lay still in her arms. Cold. Already. Stamata wept over him. Kissing his forehead and cheeks, she repeated her prayer in a shaky voice. 'God look after him. My son. Take my son to heaven. God, look after him. My angel. God, please.' She hugged the small body tight to her chest. 'I love you, Elias. My son. My son. Be with God now. I will meet you in heaven,' she broke down.

~

20.5 kilometres

It was an uncanny resemblance. Stamata rubbed her eyes. The boy took a few steps back. Stamata knelt. 'Hello. Thank you for coming out. Sorry if I frightened you. You look just like my son.' A tear escaped her left eye and trickled down her cheek. Stamata swiped at it with the back of her hand. 'What's your name?' she asked. The boy made a gesture towards the tree. Then he pointed at his throat and shook his head. 'You can't talk?' Stamata asked. The boy shook his head and looked at the ground. 'Oh. That's okay. I bet you still know the way to Athens from here. The big city. Can you show me?' Stamata put out her hand. The boy hesitated. 'If you show me, I have a little gift for you.' Stamata removed a small coin from the leather purse she had tied into her top and showed it to him. 'For your mama?' The boys' eyes ballooned as he took in the coin. He looked around. Then he took Stamata's hand. She rose to her feet and he pulled her gently back to the fence. 'Thank you,' she said. They climbed through and the boy took her hand once more. He began to run, leading Stamata back along the road she'd just come. At the intersection he pointed down the road to the left of where Stamata had originally come. 'Are you sure?' she asked the boy. 'To the city, to Athens?'

He nodded his head vigorously.

'Thank you. I'm glad I found you. Or you found me. Eli ... kind child. Here, give this to your mama.' Stamata held the coin out. The boy looked at his feet. 'Please, take it. You've earned it.' The boy took the coin and shoved it deep in his pocket. He grinned widely at Stamata, then waved and ran off. Back down his road. Stamata watched until he disappeared from view. She took a deep breath and started running in the direction he'd shown her.

34 kilometres

The sun had moved deeper to the west and was now blinding her. The heat of the day had passed but Stamata's cheeks remained crimson. She kept a steady pace and focused on the ground in front. 'I am strong. I will finish.' She repeated this mantra over and over. The scenery moved slowly past. Her legs were sore and the pain that radiated from her hips reminded her of being heavily pregnant. She grimaced and felt every footfall. She gazed into the distance, trying to shift her focus away from the pain. The trees gave way to farmhouses dotted along the lonely road.

38 kilometres

'You've done it, Stamata,' she whispered to herself when she realised she was in the outskirts of Athens. She smiled and looked around her. As she entered a busier street, she saw a small group of men milling on the side of the road. 'You're a disgrace and you bring shame to your family,' one of the men yelled at her, shaking his fist in the air. Stamata stopped smiling and kept running, faster. The jeering spurred her on. 'I'll show them,' she muttered under her breath. 'I am strong, I will finish!' Tears sprang at her eyes when she saw it. Far away in the distance. Panathenaic Stadium sat between the hills of

Ardettos and Agra. At first, she tried to swallow the emotion, biting hard on the side of her lip. Then she gave in and let the tears stream down her face. As she neared the entrance to the stadium grounds, she put her hand to her chest. 'This is for you my darling Elias. I honour your memory. I miss you. I love you, forever,' she panted.

40 kilometres

Stamata only saw the guards when she was nearly upon them.

'Halt,' one commanded, raising his hand high to signal his words. She stopped abruptly. 'No women are allowed onto the field of the stadium,' the other said.

'But I'm a runner. I've come from Marathónas, I've just run a marathon.'

'The marathon was yesterday,' the first guard scoffed. 'Women are forbidden from entering the games of the first Olympiad.'

'What does it matter whether I am a woman or a man. I ran the same track from Marathónas this morning that the men ran yesterday, to stand before you here in Athens. I am a person. I ran. And now I will finish.' Stamata moved forward, but the guards blocked her path.

'You are a woman. And women are forbidden,' the second guard said.

'Right. Well. I want to see Philamon,' Stamata said. 'And get him to change this ridiculous rule.'

The guards stood silent.

'As the National Guard, will you bear witness to the day and time that I stand before you?' Stamata asked.

'Well, arr ...' The first guard looked to the second, who raised his eyebrows in response.

'Here,' Stamata said, pulling a neatly folded piece of

paper out of her leather purse. She wiped the sweat from her hand and unfolded the paper. It was a handwritten note stating the date, Stamata's name, hometown, and the time she had left Marathónas, signed by a local police officer and witnessed by the banker. 'Sign here, please. And note the date and time.' Stamata pointed to the space near 'arrived in Athens'.

The first guard drew out a pen from his blazer pocket. He leant over and used his thigh as a rest. He wrote the date, time and his name before scrawling his signature.

'Thank you. You too.' She gestured to the second guard. He rolled his eyes then took the paper and pen from his colleague and added his name and signature.

'Off with you now,' the guard said, handing back the paper to Stamata and waiving his hand. She turned and walked away, folding the paper and placing it carefully back in the leather purse. She looked at the stadium. She started to jog once more, very slowly. She followed the road that circled the proud landmark until she was back at the entrance gate. As she made her surrogate lap of honour, she pictured the crowd inside the stadium, cheering her on. She collapsed on the grass outside the entrance, exhausted. The pain in her legs and hips now emanated throughout her body. There was no part of her that didn't hurt.

43 kilometres
'Philamon will see you now.'

Stamata stood and hobbled into the office after the short man.

'Miss Stamata Revithi,' he announced to the suited gentleman.

'How can I help you Miss Revithi?'

140

'I ran the marathon today. I'd like to have my time recorded.'

'That's impossible. No women are permitted to run the marathon. The race was yesterday.'

'Well, I ran it anyway. I began at the starting line in Marathónas this morning. Although I think I got lost at one point and had to backtrack. So, I'm sure I went even further than 40 kilometres.'

'Do you have any proof?'

'Yes, of course,' Stamata said, presenting the unfolded note to the man. He studied it, running his thumb and forefinger through his thick moustache.

'I see. Well it appears you did complete the distance although these signatures would have to be verified. However, I still can't record your time as you didn't compete in the race.'

'Women can do it, sir. They can run just like me. You must change the rule, I'm begging you. Let women run too. Let them know the freedom of running along the road and the achievement of finishing a marathon.'

'I will have to consider this,' he said standing. 'Right now, I have another appointment. Good day, Miss Revithi.'

44 kilometres

Stamata turned off the main street away from the setting sun. A carriage drove past, heading into the centre of Athens. Dust rose from the sandy road. Her tall, slim, dishevelled figure disappeared into the dust.

References

Nix, E 2020, *Why is a marathon 26.2 miles*, A&E Television Networks, viewed 21 June 2020, https://www.history.com/news/why-is-a-marathon-26-2-miles.

Runningheroes 2018, Stamata Revithi: Marathon Woman, runningheroes, viewed 21 June 2020, https://uk.runningheroes.com/en/blog/marathon-woman.

Tarasouleas, A 2018, *Stamata Revithi, "Alias Melpomeni"*, Olympic World Library, viewed 21 June 2020, https://library.olympic.org/Default/doc/SYRACUSE/353009/stamata-revithi-alias-melpomeni-by-athanasios-tarasouleas.

Wikipedia 2019, *Stamata Revithi*, viewed 21 June 2020, https://en.wikipedia.org/wiki/Stamata_Revithi.

Ernie
Rainie Zenith

My lover is dying.

We met late, both forty-two, both Elvis diehards, both into hiking through spectacular scenery in remote locations. The Inca Trail was endless shambolic staircases, an acute episode of food poisoning, and the coming together of two akin spirits. The priceless reward for such a brutal trek was not the breathtaking abandoned citadel of Machu Picchu, but the unparalleled joyful finality of discovering one's soulmate.

We would go on to explore the planet together, trekking its tallest peaks hand in hand, from Tanzania to Tibet. We devoted hours of the working week to running and biking in preparation for the extreme elevations we would encounter during our annual high-altitude expeditions. He and I crafted aerobic capacities to rival that of any Olympian; our bodies specialised in the ultra-efficient oxygenation of red blood cells.

How mercilessly ironic for him to be dying due to the failure of his lungs to provide him with sufficient oxygen.

My lover is dying of acute respiratory distress.

My lover, the man whose embrace evokes in me both a comforting familiarity like a ticking clock to a weaned pup, and a stoking of the flames of passion as though our romance were freshly forged. I know the coordinates of his every last crease and mole, could scrunch my eyes and trace his outline in precise detail, have learnt by heart the exact sag of his stomach, bulge of his biceps, sharp lines of his shinbones.

His body is not new, but we all know where beauty lies, and to this beholder it is a work of art encasing his precious soul; together they manifest as my fiercely cherished life partner.

Our love is not new either, yet it remains a vibrant shade of magenta. Never did it pale to pink, or worse yet, fade away entirely.

My lover is my heaven, my haven, my home.

My lover is dying in the hospital, alone.

Prior to this surreal era, we traversed a good portion of the globe together, though a number of further-flung destinations – Reykjavík, Tenerife, Rapa Nui – are yet to be struck off the bucket list. They shall remain forever unstruck; what was once a potential future is now a wistful fantasy doomed to the confines of my grief-stricken imagination.

It was rare for either of us to travel alone, but with my mother's recent ailing health, we agreed it was best I stay home while my lover journeyed to London to meet his newest nephew.

We weren't to know he would be swept up in the middle of a pandemic and struggle to catch a return flight. We weren't to know that upon landing he would commence a fortnight of hotel quarantine only to be diagnosed with coronavirus four days in. We weren't to know his dry cough would deteriorate into a wet one and he would be hospitalised one week later.

My ardent anticipation of a joyful reunion crumbled to ashes on a forgotten hearth, bone-cold and empty.

~

The hospital is only fifteen kilometres from home, but it may as well be on Mars. I cannot go there, cannot see him, cannot touch him. I hadn't seen him in two months, since he kissed me farewell at the airport with star-sprinkled eyes, eager to meet the new baby, reunite with his brother, discover more of London; to go, do, live.

Then I got the call, far too early in the day. I was still in bed, still sleeping on my own side, even if my lover was not there to occupy the other. By keeping out of his space, I could somehow pretend that he was in it, right where he belonged.

They had commenced palliative care, the nurse said. They didn't expect him to see the other side of the weekend, she said.

His side of the bed would remain empty forever.

Its vastness was suddenly overwhelming, and I jettisoned myself from beneath the warm covers to collapse on the hardwood floor.

The nurse's voice continued to flow. I was invited to come to the hospital and see him.

To see him!

I arrived almost before she had hung up.

~

My phone, my watch, my glasses were to be left in the car. My temperature was to be normal, my flu vaccination to be current, my name to be signed at the bottom of a lengthy disclaimer form. A nurse would supervise my donning of the required protective equipment, beginning with a white mask for my face and a net to restrain my hair. My first attempt at putting on the mask was deemed incorrect, and I was compelled to toss it into an overflowing bin and start over with a new one. Then sanitise my hands. Put on surgical booties to cover my shoes. Then sanitise my hands. Put on full body smock, sanitise hands. Then on with a plastic face shield and two pairs of latex gloves for good measure. I was done up like an astronaut, ready to enter an alien land.

The nurse led me through plastic-sheeted halls to my lover's ward, told me I had exactly fifteen minutes, and warned me I may find the experience confronting. I was bursting out of my skin to see him, yet I was also apprehensive. This was the last time I would ever get to spend with him. This was so special, so bittersweet, so momentous; I wanted nothing to go wrong. I stepped through the doorway.

My lover was lying on a hospital bed. I was allowed no closer than one and a half metres.

His eyes were open.

His skin was grey.

His head, my lover's sweet darling head, lolled to one side at an awkward angle.

He is on morphine, the nurse told me.

The man who held my heart was reduced to this broken, pitiful being before me. The man I had chosen to share my life with was slipping through the veil between this world and the next. The man in whose eyes I had always sought and found reassurance was trembling and feverish, and I could not comfort him. There was to be no touching, no proximity of any kind.

I spoke to him lovingly, soothingly, repeatedly, then as he failed to respond, urgently. Hidden beneath a mask and gown, I called to him, eyes welling upon the realisation.

He did not recognise me.

His breath was a rattlesnake, and when it burst into a fit of coughing the nurse whisked me from the room, allowing re-entry only once his breathing had stabilised.

I gazed forlornly at what was left of the man I loved, a crippled shell and woozy mind no longer fit to house his noble soul. The one with whom I had lain a thousand times was departing his earthbound vessel, was beyond my reach, beyond even my voice.

'It's time to go,' the nurse said.

I could barely choke out a final farewell.

'Goodbye, my love.'

I don't know if he heard me.

~

We should have been attending my niece's wedding in Adelaide in December. Her mother, my sister, lost her husband two years ago, to a long battle with a brain tumour. She had to watch him slowly wither and decay over a period of many months. She was at his side from the time of diagnosis right through to the time of relinquishing her job to bathe, feed and wipe him like a baby. When he was finally dealt the mercy of death, she was at his bedside, playing him a soft score of his favourite tunes, stroking, soothing, whispering goodbye.

Would anyone play the King's records for my lover, a soundtrack to his egress?

As I sit at home, numb with not knowing, my lover is erupting in pink secretions from the blood cells leaking into his airways. I crave news of his condition, yet dread it. He is drowning in his own fluids.

I miss him. I don't think I can live without him.

We should have been celebrating his birthday with sponge cake in September, planting the garden with tomatoes in October, toasting our anniversary with moscato in November.

Instead, he is dying.

The two decades we spent in a divine state of oneness feel like an eternity, for I cannot remember what my life was like prior to his entering it. An eternity that was not long enough, as I dread to imagine a life without him, having known him, loved him, cherished him every day for the past twenty years.

How grateful I am for each priceless minute he and I were blessed with one another's company. From those budding moments high in the Andes through to mundane evenings in living room silence, from the long Sunday afternoons of exuberant lovemaking to the hurried little goodbye pecks on the way out the door on work mornings; I am thankful for it all.

The manner in which this joy has all ended leaves me like the ruin of a war-torn city, lovelorn for its ill-fated citizens whose memories stalk the streets in the absence of their earthly bodies.

We all must one day die; certain knowledge of this is the penalty for being born human. While a premature emptying of the hourglass feels as though one has been short-changed, no-one can know when their final grains of time will pass.

I am not bitter that the man I love more than I ever thought possible must depart this world so soon. But I am devastated I cannot be with him when he does.

My lover is dying, and I can't even hold his hand.

About the Authors

Sasha Buntman

Sasha Buntman is passionate about communicating, organising, digital marketing and independent publishing. Her purpose in life has always revolved around the art of organising. Organising the layout of elements on your page or in your book; organising words, sentences and messages together to create something meaningful and worthwhile for your audience.

As the founder of Midnight Media, Sasha provides affordable self-publishing solutions for fiction and non-fiction. Sasha project manages everything for you and ensures that your self-publishing journey runs smoothly and successfully.

Copywriting is another obsession of Sasha's. Her subsidiary business, Midnight Marketing, provides digital marketing support services to authors and entrepreneurs: including email, website and social media content management; copywriting; advertising and more.

Mube Akinci-Desem

Mube's passion for writing is a life-long affair; she used to write little short stories and 1-2 verse poems during primary school. Her articles, short stories and poems have been published in newspapers and anthologies and she is in the process of having her first book published.

Mube likes to read historical and science fiction novels. Her love of travelling and thirst for different cultures has taken her around the world to some of the most unexpected places in Europe and Asia. Mube also loves to sit and enjoy cups of coffee with friends in cosmopolitan coffee shops around Melbourne. Mube enjoys walking, sometimes her long walks may extend as far as the CBD.

Ingrid Fry

Ingrid is the author of the soon to be published Crystal Sphere series—a set of speculative fiction thrillers set in Australia—and two self-illustrated children's books. An astrologer who prepared her chart many years ago said, 'your destiny is to be either a nun, or a writer'. For Ingrid, the choice was a no-brainer, even though writing sometimes makes her feel as cloistered as a nun.

A writer, business development consultant, and minder of a husband and a beagle with super-powers, she lives in a leafy suburb on the outskirts of Melbourne. When she's not writing, you can find her pistol shooting at the local gun club, dancing her socks off at The Caravan Music Club, or being a passionate karateka, inching ever closer to a black belt in karate.

Sakuntala Gananathan

Sakuntala is a retired chartered accountant. Her historical novel *White Flowers of Yesterday* was published in the US and was awarded Editor's Choice by her publishers, iUniverse Inc.

An excerpt of their appraisal: 'The author has done a fantastic job of weaving setting, characterisation, historical information, dialogue and plot together to create a complete, unique and compelling story...' while Kirkus Review wrote '...a surfeit of grace and wit...'

Sakuntala takes an active interest in the Tamil Senior Citizens Fellowship (Victoria) Inc, a non-profit association. She is also a member of the Australian Tamil Literary and Arts Society Inc., Casey Tamil Manram, and Tamil Senior Citizen Benevolent Society, all based in Victoria. In 2013 her short story, 'Mend a Bend', earned her a prize at the Monash Word Fest Short Story Competition.

Ruth Kweitel

Ruth Kweitel was a registered nurse and psychologist in her professional life. She spent most of her employment working as a registered nurse, the last 25 years in mental health. In the latter years of her employment, she worked as a psychology tutor at a university in Melbourne until she fully retired. As part of her retirement, she developed an interest in creative writing as a hobby and subsequently began writing short stories instead of the textbook she had intended to write, when she completed her PhD. Ruth gets her inspiration from the environment and social issues.

Marlene Laurent

Born in Australia, Marlene grew up in the post war suburb of South Oakleigh. Brought up a Catholic she entered the convent at the age of 17 after attending boarding school in Fremantle WA. She left the convent following the Ecumenical Council when changes were implemented in the Catholic Church.

She worked in an office in South Melbourne for a short time where she met her husband Jim. Soon after she went to Toorak Teacher's college and completed a teaching degree. Later she studied to add to her qualifications completing a Bachelor of Teaching and an ED Admin certificate. She taught at Brighton Primary before having her daughter Monica and Noble Park Primary on her return from family leave.

Teaching became a passion. She was actively involved in education in the Victorian system and implemented many changes to the curriculum during her career. She became an Assistant Principal at Brandon Park Primary and then Principal at Oakwood Park Primary and finally at Glenferrie Primary. She played basketball and tennis and attended the gym regularly to keep fit.

On retiring she decided to have a go at writing, something she had always thought of doing. She is a member of the Caulfield Writer's Group and the Monash Writer's group. This short story is her fourth for Monash Writer's group anthologies. She wrote her first short story for *View from the Hill*. Her second short story *What a Coincidence* was written for the *First Line* and her third, *We can Still be Friends* for the *Last Line*.

Marlene Lives in East Bentleigh and spends her time cycling, keeping fit at the local gym, reading, writing and travelling. She is member of the Australian Conservation Association, The Wilderness Society and other conservation groups. She takes an interest in her local community, as Secretary of the Glen Eira Residents Association.

Sung-Ju Suya Lee

Suya received a BFA from York University, Canada, an MBA from Bradford University School of Management, UK, and a PhD in Media & Communication from RMIT University, Australia. As part of her creative practice PhD, she wrote a farce comedy screenplay, which was long-listed for the ScreenCraft Comedy screenplay contest. One of her short stories was short-listed for the inaugural Apollo Writers Festival short story contest.

Besides being a student and travelling, she has had many 'day' jobs to support her writing, filmmaking and acting career. She feels privileged to be a part of the Monash Writers Group.

Andrew Marmont

Andrew Marmont was born in Auckland, New Zealand, and fell in love with Rugby League when the Auckland Warriors joined the ARL competition in 1995.

A regular contributor to Big League, the official NRL magazine, he also writes for Inside Sport, Rugby League World and Commentary Box Sports. Andrew has loved sport from an early age, frequently airing his views on NZ's Radio Sport as a boy. His first interview was Sir Edmund Hillary at the age of 13.

Andrew is the author of *Their Finest Hour: A History of the Rugby League World Cup in 10 Matches*.

Bala Mudaly

Bala Mudaly was born in South Africa and migrated with his wife to Australia thirty years ago. He retired as a psychologist from Monash Health in Dec 2018 at the age of 80. His debut collection of poems and short stories set in Australia, *Colours of Hope and Despair*, was published in 2018. He's also had a short story, 'Self-Inflected Pain of the Writer's Kind', published in the *Victorian Writer*.

Dedicated to learning and mastering the art of creative writing, Bala is now trying his hand at creative non-fiction. He's now in the final stages of completing his memoir, provisionally titled Colour-coated Identities: Growing up Indian South African.

Robert New

Robert has spent too much of his life studying and has earned seven tertiary qualifications. Robert has degrees in psychology, sociology, biology and education, all of which inspire his writing, which has been described as 'educational of the human condition', and 'smart and imaginative'.

Robert's books include *Incite Insight*, *MoveMind* and *Colours of Death: Sergeant Thomas' Casebook*. He recently signed a publishing deal for his next novel, *Sovereign Assassin*. Robert has chaired the Monash Writers Group since 2017.

Robert is mildly kosmemophobic – meaning he has a fear of jewellery. He has no idea why.

When he was in high school, a dare escalated a little too quickly and Robert made the state final in an interpretive dance competition.

Andy Russell

Over most of his working life Andy Russell was involved with research into intelligent robotics. Some of his robots communicated using puffs of air, licked the floor to follow chemical trails or burrowed through the ground searching for chemical leaks. It was not uncommon for reviewers of his research to complain it was too speculative, perhaps too much like science fiction? Now, in retirement, he has the freedom to explore robotics and science fiction more broadly without any requirement to demonstrate practical implementations.

His debut novel *Intelligent Consent* was released in 2020.

Gordon J R Smith

Gordon J R Smith was born in 1927 in Victoria. He qualified as a tradesman fitter and turner in 1949 with the Victorian Railways. He was a Rover Scout and member of the Youth Hostels Association. In 1952 he sailed abroad to the UK on a working and backpacking holiday, returning to Australia in 1953. He worked, married and raised a family on the Kiewa Hydro-Electric Scheme for 10 years. Returning to Melbourne, he worked for 18 years with General Electric. When GE closed, he taught Fluid Power at the Royal Melbourne Institute of Technology, from where he retired in 1993. He has written and published books about his travels abroad and working life.

Erica Tippett

Erica's love of story was developed as a child and she has fond memories of her dad reading bedtime stories every night. An aspiring writer, she was reminded by the passing of her dad that life is too short to just talk about the things you want to do; and has now written a book that she hopes to publish soon. Erica has always had a keen interest in all things international and hopes to promote diversity of voice and perspectives through an upcoming writing project. She loves descriptive writing that gives the reader a true sense of place, and transports them somewhere new.

Rainie Zenith

Rainie Zenith is a Melbourne-based author with a penchant for pieces that fall broadly within the gothic fantasy realm. Her stories have appeared in numerous anthologies such as *Tales of Blood* and *Squalor* from Dark Cloud Press, and *Autumn's Harvest* from Fantasia Divinity. She is also a singer-songwriter. Find out more at facebook.com/rainiezenith or rainiezenith.com

Her contribution to this anthology, Ernie, won the 2020 Monash Wordfest competition.

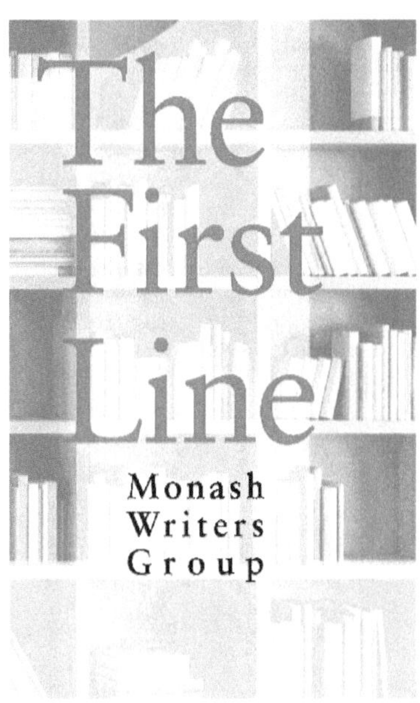

This is a short story anthology by the Monash Writers Group. Each writer has taken the **first** line of a story they like and used it as the starting point for a new tale. Some lines are famous, others obscure, but the works they have inspired are original and entertaining.

From historical fiction, drama, science fiction, mystery, adventure and literary there is a story in this collection for every reader.

ISBN 9780648327332

Available to order from bookshops and online retailers including Amazon.com.
https://amzn.to/2oNicDj

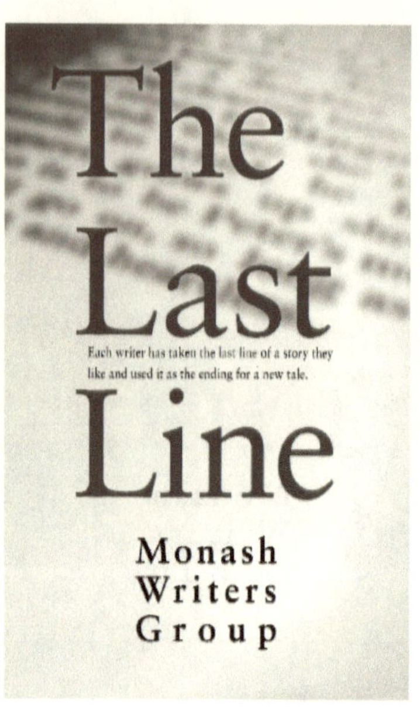

This is a short story anthology by the Monash Writers Group. Each writer has taken the **last** line of a story they like and used it as the ending for a new tale. Some lines are famous, others obscure, but the works they have inspired are original and entertaining.

From historical fiction, speculative fiction, mystery, adventure and literary there is a story in this collection for every reader.

ISBN 9780648327394
Available to order from bookshops and online retailers including Amazon.com.
https://amzn.to/37mavXa